SYNCHRONICITY
The Story of Anna

CONSTANCE FLAMION

ISBN: 1517501644
ISBN: 13: 978-1517501648
Library of Congress Control number: 2015916048

CreateSpace Independent Publishing Platform
North Charleston, SC

The views expressed in this novel do not necessarily reflect those of its author. This book is a work of fiction. Names, characters, places, and incidents are either a product of my imagination or are used fictitiously. Any resemblance to actual persons, living or dead, or events is entirely coincidental.

Cover design by Robin Ludwig Design Inc.

Acknowledgements

I would like to personally thank my editor Susan Krawitz who's insight and guidance kept my literary train moving smoothly down the tracks. Writing my first novel, I was filled with anxious dread that my writing would come off as jumbled mix of both amateurish composition and a nightmarish look at how you butcher the English language. Susan truly made me believe in myself as a writer.

The mistakes in this book are mine alone. Anything that is deemed funny, logical, heart-warming or brilliant, I'll take credit for that as well.

Parts of this book have my characters using American Sign Language (ASL). In the storyline, ASL, is written out as proper English. ASL is a visual language. There is significant differences between signed and spoken languages. My writing it as proper English was my own interpretation on how I made my story flow. If I have offended anyone by this, I apologize.

Thanks to my family, especially Tom & Virginia Lay, for their unwavering support while I wrote this book.

Additionally, I wish to give heartfelt acknowledgements to my children Angela Flamion, Phillip Flamion, II and Alexandra Flamion Hershberger for their incredibly humbling love and support during the very trying time it took to write this book. Not once did that stop believing in my ability to finish it. I hope my finishing this book proves to the three of them that it's never too late to go after their dreams.

This book is dedicated in loving memory for:

Phillip J. Flamion

Gayle H. Flamion

Timothy E. Lay

James R. Lay

Timothy E. Lay, II

Shane M. Lay

"No one truly dies if you keep them in your heart and memories forever. Let those memories of moments of love, laughter, tears and joy live on in the thoughts and actions of your everyday lives. Let their stories continue on in your children and grandchildren and all that come after."

- SYNCHRONICITY *The Story of Anna*

For my precious granddaughter:

Persaeus Rose

May you always have a story to tell.

SYNCHRONICITY
The Story of Anna

CHAPTER ONE
DECEMBER 12, 2012
12:12 P.M.

It was raining the morning that Anna Anderson disappeared in the middle of a car accident. It was a cold December day, two weeks before Christmas Eve, and the rain was coming down in icy gray sheets. The small town of Greenway, Indiana was decorated for Christmas. Snowmen and reindeer and fat plastic Santa's adorned every storefront window on the town's festive main street. Christmas lights twinkled from every tree and light post, visible this day even at noon because of the overcast sky. The wind played havoc with the umbrellas and shopping bags of those who had braved the weather to come out to lunch or purchase holiday gifts and carried the sound of Christmas music, piped in from the National bank on the corner. The classic brick Prairie School architecture, spoke of years past. It could have been a Currier & Ives post card painting of small town America.

That was why the accident at the intersection of Main Street and Third Avenue was such a shock to everyone who heard and witnessed it. The horrendous noise of two vehicles colliding, a sound that makes the hearts of everyone who hears it pause just for a moment and think, *"Oh, God! I hope that wasn't anyone I know!"* But, one of the vehicles did indeed contain someone many knew very well.

Jane Monroe's red two-door sedan now sat idle in the middle of the intersection, the passenger side crumpled from the force of impact, the mangled metal seemingly attached to the black SUV that had skidded through a red light in the driving rain and was now at a smoking rest. Both of the passenger side windows on the sedan were cracked and broken, pieces of tinted glass strewn across the wet pavement like dirty ice cubes.

Some of the onlookers rushed to the vehicles to help as others called 911. Jane Monroe was unconscious behind the steering wheel of the sedan. Her face was covered by the imploded air bag, blood running in crimson rivulets down her cheeks and over her tan winter coat. One of the by-standers hurriedly checked for a pulse on Jane's neck. He could feel it beating frantically through her damp skin. "It's Jane Monroe!" called out the by-stander. "Someone call Eddie!"

***

Edward "Eddie" Monroe was the police chief of Greenway and had been for more than sixteen years. A Gulf War veteran and former Marine, he'd been born in nineteen fifty-seven in the small Indiana community just a thirty minute drive northwest of Indianapolis, and raised there. The town was surrounded by cornfields and large farms, cow pastures and the occasional Amish buggy parked in the driveways of white farm houses. It was a place where people used to leave their doors unlocked at night, but over the years the big city crime had also come to Greenway, albeit at a much slower pace. Robberies and vandalism and calls to break up a domestic argument were frequent now with the downturn in the economy and stress over unemployment that had hit the whole county hard. However, in Eddie's 16 years as chief, there had been only one murder in the small town.

When the call came, Eddie was already on the phone. A handsome man whose face was lined with what his wife Jane called "wisdom lines". He had dark hair streaked with gray and deep set blue eyes that carried a look of intelligence and knowledge he had accumulated over his fifty-five years. He wore a white buttoned shirt and blue tie in contrast to the relaxed jeans on his long legs, his booted feet draped over the corner of his wooden desk.

"Mrs. Carson, I told you already that I can't arrest him for anything," he said as he looked over at Lieutenant Mark Browning who sat at his own desk doing paperwork. "Being lazy isn't a crime, Mary Jo. Just go out there and talk to him." He listened for a minute, then said, "No...do not do that either!" He shook his head. "I don't want to have to arrest *you*! I'm pretty sure a head bashing by frying pan is still domestic assault." Eddie rubbed his temples as he hung up the phone. It had been a long week but it was finally getting close to the weekend. Not that he ever got much rest. Being police chief was a twenty-four hour job.

He glanced over at Mark as the phone rang again. When Mark picked it up, he got up to stretch his legs and look out the window at the pouring rain. The clouds above the trees were ominous and the sight of them gave him a chill just for a moment. He closed his eyes. It was only just past noon time and it had already been a very tiring day. He turned around to get coffee and found that Mark was staring right at him.

"Eddie, it's Jane," Mark said bluntly. "There was an accident. They're in route to the hospital. I am going to drive you there right now," When he'd finished, Eddie stood rooted to the floor holding his coffee cup as if it was some kind of lifeline.

* * *

Jane Monroe was taken by ambulance to Greenway Community Hospital. She was still unconscious as they brought her in and the team of emergency personnel began to work on her. Visually, there was a lot of blood from what looked like a broken nose and facial lacerations, likely from the inflated airbag. She began to gain consciousness as the doctors and nurses evaluated her. Jane heard vaguely through the fog in her head the voice of her husband Eddie,

3

asking for her, and the raised voices of others, people she did not know, trying to calm him. She tried hard to think...to remember what had happened. Her head hurt. Nothing came to her but a black wall of nothingness. Finally, she gave up and let the drugs do their work and drifted off into a fitful slumber.

Eddie sat next to Jane holding her small hand as she slept on the cot in the E.R. He loved this woman he had been married to for thirty years with all his heart. They had been high school sweethearts. He'd joined the Marines after graduating and she'd gone to Purdue to study botany and now owned her own floral shop. She had been with him through everything; his service during the Gulf War, training in the academy and the ups and downs of being a police officer, and the death of both his parents. They were never blessed with children but so blessed with each other that he had no regrets with the way their lives had unfolded. He sat looking at her injured face, still so beautiful to him and he said a silent prayer of thanks that she wasn't more seriously hurt. They were still waiting for her to be taken for x-rays but it looked like she would be fine. He felt a squeeze around his heart as he held back the tears that threatened to spill down his rugged face.

Once Eddie had composed himself he left Jane to talk to Mark Browning and the emergency paramedics that brought Jane in. He had been driven there in such a hurry and in such a mental fog that he did not question Mark much and had gotten only the vaguest of answers about the accident.

"Hey, Mark," he called out as he approached his lieutenant. "Where did they bring Anna to?"

Mark looked at him oddly. "Anna? Your sister; Anna?" he asked, as though puzzled by this question.

"Yes, my sister Anna!" Eddie said. "They were together. They went for a birthday lunch. It's Anna's 50th Birthday." The quizzical look on Mark's face made an uneasy feeling began to grow inside him. He found himself holding his breath as though waiting to be punched in the gut.

Mark took Eddie's arm as he guided him down the hospital hallway to the small waiting room. He sat him down on the worn couch and shook his head.

"Eddie, she must have gotten out before the accident," he said as though puzzled. "No one was in the car except Jane."

CHAPTER TWO

Eddie stood up and looked at Mark incredulously.

"I don't understand," he said, shaking his head. "She had to have been in the car with her. Jane called me after she picked Anna up from work and told me they were on their way to lunch. That was less than 20 minutes before the accident."

"Look, Eddie, maybe she dropped her off some place for a moment. The bank or pharmacy... or somewhere beforehand," Mark said. "We'll find her. I'll talk to the emergency workers again and question all the witnesses personally." Mark reached for his cell phone.

Eddie rushed back to the E.R. cubicle where Jane lay on the bed waiting to be taken to Radiology for her x-rays. She was moving around a bit more than she had first been when he saw her. Eddie leaned down to stroke her dark hair.

"Jane, sweetheart. It's Eddie," he said as he touched her gently. "Can you hear me? Baby, you're going to be OK. Do you remember what happened?"

Hearing her husband call her name made Jane begin to stir. As she concentrated on the sound of his voice, it began to bring her out of her gray fog. Finally, she opened her eyes and looked up to see her husband gazing down tenderly at her.

She became more aware of her surroundings. She was in a hospital cubicle with emergency equipment, and the steady beeping sound of the EKG machine. She noticed an I.V. attached to one slim hand. Clinching her eyes against the pain in her head, she tried to remember how she had gotten here.

"I...it was raining and cold...freezing. The rain was coming down so hard. It was difficult to see out the window. I had the defroster going. I remember I had to take off my gloves to turn it on," Jane said. "Isn't that a strange thing to remember?"

"Honey, do you remember where you were going?" Eddie asked.

Jane sat quietly for a moment, trying to think. "It's Anna's birthday. I picked her up at work and we were going to her favorite restaurant," she paused. "Marcos Place, the one downtown off Main Street. Oh my God! Anna! Is she hurt?"

"Shhh, shhh Jane, it's all right," he said as he tried to calm his agitated wife. "Anna was in the car with you, is that what you are saying?"

Jane furrowed her brow and looked up at him.

"Of course she was in the car with me! I told you I had just picked her up from the library. I even called you on your cell and told you! I...we were talking about her birthday and being fifty...she made a joke...I can't remember what now, but I remember we were both laughing," she said as she touched his hand. "Then, the intersection came up, the one with the bank on the corner...and the light was green...I drove through it and..." she sighed. "I don't remember after that."

Eddie sat down heavily in the chair beside her hospital bed. Anna had been in the car. How could that be? Where was his sister?

***

Eddie left the hospital and drove back to the scene of the accident. The street was closed off while his officers talked to witnesses, took pictures, and cleaned up the crash site. Eddie got out of his car and questioned the people standing around. He told his officers to start looking for Anna, who was presumed missing at that point. Mark was gathering evidence, calling her co-workers and friends and interviewing witnesses. When Eddie was finished with the witnesses, he drove out to Anna's colonial home on the outskirts of town and did his own frantic search of the premises. He knew that her silver Toyota was at Ellis Garage getting a new transmission this week. She had gotten a ride to work from a co-worker and it was the reason Jane had picked her up. Eddie had called the garage himself and was told they were still working on the car. He called Mark and ordered him to issue an APB immediately. Anna had to be somewhere!

Eddie saw part of his job as a Police Chief's as knowing every single family that lived in his town. He was aware of every small misdemeanor, from vagrancy and public intoxication to petty theft and disorderly conduct. He was aware of every citation written and of course, the more serious crimes that he personally oversaw. He also knew families on a socially intimate level. Those that he talked to as he walked the streets of Greenway and went to church with, the men he fished with on the Wabash River, those that he had gone to high school with, and some he had followed into the military. He had witnessed accidents and shootings, broken up fights and consoled family members after natural deaths and suicides and kept down the contents of his stomach while viewing the autopsy of the only murder victim in all his years as chief. He'd spent 12 years in the military and thought he was prepared to see it all.

An hour later, the sight of his wife's red sedan nearly brought him to his knees. Standing there in the police garage while the lab technicians worked over the car and made notes, Eddie felt his insides clinch with an iron fist of apprehension as he gazed upon the wreckage. The beautiful car which had been a gift to Jane for their 30th anniversary last summer, now sat parked at a haphazard angle, looking like a large toy that had been dropped on its side and stomped by some giant angry child. The whole passenger side was caved in so badly that the car barely resembled a vehicle that had ever been drivable.

He walked over to Elaine Miles, the field technician who was standing by the wrecked car, taking notes. She stood to look at him as he approached, her brown eyes dark with concern.

"How is Jane doing, Chief?" she asked.

"She's going to be alright, thanks," Eddie said, and sighed heavily. "Elaine, can you tell me at all if there was evidence of anyone else in this car besides my wife, at the time of the accident?"

Elaine frowned, "I know there was only one victim pulled from the wreckage and that was Jane," she said.

"Yes, I know what was reported. I am asking you if there is *any* evidence that there was anyone else in the car at the time of the accident? Is there any physical body trauma noted on the passenger side...blood for instance or an injury..." his voice trailed off.

"We only noted trauma on the driver's side, likely from Jane. There was blood on the deflated airbag and a small amount on the side door and ceiling as well. The passenger side is very smashed in, as you can see," she said, indicating the area with one hand, "But, there is no evidence that anyone else was in the car with her."

Elaine had never seen her boss act so strangely. The man who was always the voice of reason was asking her questions that did not make any sense.

"Tell me what's going on, Eddie," she said.

Instead of responding, Eddie walked around the car slowly, trying to look at it from a impersonal point of view. And then he tried to see the accident in his head, the impact of the two vehicles at the intersection. The driver of the black SUV was not hurt. He had been taken to jail, dazed and smelling slightly of alcohol according to the police report. Mark had questioned him at the jail a while ago.

"It's my sister Anna's birthday," he said at last. "She and Jane were going to lunch to celebrate it. We were having a party for her tomorrow night at our house," he said. "Jane called me after she picked up Anna from work to let me know how the weather was. I was worried about them being out in it. Everything was fine. They were on their way to the restaurant," he paused. "Both of them. Jane

9

insists that Anna was in the car with her when this happened." He looked at Elaine, showing lines of worry on his handsome face.

Elaine looked at him quizzically for a moment then bent down towards something from a box on the floor. She looked at Eddie carefully. "We did find two purses in the car. We found one stuck under the passenger seat. I looked inside and it could belong Anna," she said, as she handed Eddie a black leather handbag.

He slowly took it from her. He recognized the silver buckle with an "A" attached to the front of the bag instantly. He sat the bag down on the table and unzipped it. He peered inside and pulled out the black wallet and opened it. For a long moment he stood there looking at his sister's photo. Her lovely face framed with dark blonde hair that fell in waves past her shoulders. Her blue eyes, so much like his, like their mother Maria's, stared at him. As she always did, her face wore a half smile like she was going to break into a story or joke, teasing him the way she always had since she was a little girl. He carefully lifted the driver's license that clearly showed her name. *Anna Beth Anderson.*

Eddie took the wallet and walked away from Elaine. What did it all mean? How could his sister have been in the car? There was no physical evidence or trauma caused by another person being there at the time of the accident. Could Jane be mistaken? She had a concussion, but nothing too serious. Could she indeed have dropped Anna off somewhere first like Mark had suggested? But Jane had been adamant that Anna had been sitting beside her in the passenger seat. She remembered them talking, joking. When Eddie told her they were still trying to find her sister-in-law, she'd gotten hysterical. Eddie sat there holding her as the nurse gave her a shot to calm her down until she'd fallen asleep.

Now he stood in the police garage with his head bowed, thinking back to a day 34 years earlier, when Anna was just 16 years old. She'd been a beautiful, bright, happy, full-of-life teenager. But on that day, his sister's life had come crashing down and changed forever.

CHAPTER THREE
DECEMBER 1978

Anna Monroe lay in a hospital bed surrounded by medical equipment and IV rods. The blinds were drawn and lights turned down low, and the steady beeping of the EKG machine tapping out a rhythm of the life force of the patient lying there. Eddie sat by his sister's bedside staring at her pale face and the long blonde hair lying in a tangled web around her head. Anna had been in the hospital for four days already and only gained consciousness the day before. His Mom and Dad stood outside the windowed room, talking to Anna's doctors. The sleepless nights and worry seemed to have taken a profound toll on them. He closed his eyes against the pain in his chest he felt looking at his parents. The strong front they had put up in front of Anna yesterday while giving her the news, was gone now. Their faces were drawn and haggard, making them look even older than their already advanced years.

Anna had come home sick from snow skiing in Michigan with her friends almost 10 days before. They'd gone during Christmas break to try out new skis they had all gotten as presents. What his parents first thought was just the flu, turned into something else altogether. Their brief concern about her illness blossomed into full-blown fear when they found Anna unconscious on the bathroom floor. They rushed her to the emergency room, with Eddie driving the fastest he had ever gone with his parents in the car, skidding on the icy roads and coming to a long screeching skid outside the community hospital.

When the doctor in charge called out *"She's seizing! Get the cart! She's crashing!"* in the small E.R cubicle as the staff treating Anna surrounded her, they had clutched each other's hands as though willing this young girl they all loved so much to gather her precious life-saving breath. They'd endured this for a gut-wrenching 39 seconds before the emergency staff finally stabilized her and her heart start beating again in a steady rhythm. At that point, his mother's strength had given out and her knees had buckled. Eddie and his father Bill led her to a couch in the waiting room. Eddie had stood there feeling helpless as his parents held each other and cried. None of it seemed real. He'd wiped the tears from his cheeks and sat down beside his parents, offering them his silent comfort.

Three hours later they would finally find out what was wrong with Anna. *Bacterial Meningitis.* They would have to wait an agonizing two days to see if the drugs given to her would keep her from dying, and what the side effects of the illness might be. They spent the next few days at the hospital, Eddie making runs home to get clothes and take care of the daily farm chores while his parents stayed by their daughter's side. Only when the doctors finally told them she would make it, had they been able to sleep and eat and breathe a little easier.

Anna had finally become conscious. At first confused and unaware of her surroundings, she was eventually able to focus on her family's faces. All three of them had talked to her, told her what happened and where she was, Anna looked at them blankly, not understanding, before falling back to sleep. When she was awake for more than a few minutes, she would look at them all with a puzzled expression on her pale face as they stood huddled close by her bed, quietly talking.

Finally, Anna shouted, "What is going on?" startling them all. They turned towards her and Maria moved to her bedside and took her hand.

"It's OK baby, we are just talking," she told her as she leaned down to brush Anna's blonde hair away from her forehead, something she had always done since her daughter was a toddler. Anna's eyes were huge in her pale face.

"I don't understand!" she yelled, "What are you saying?"

The doctor had tried to prepare them for this possibility. They knew there'd been a chance and it had been a silent concern. They thought they'd be ready to handle it if it did happen, but now that it quickly became apparent that it indeed had.

"I can't hear you!" Anna shouted again.

Anna was hysterical and combative, screaming until the nurse and doctors came in to calm her with a sedative. Not until they'd given her a shot, had she stopped fighting and yelling and ripping at the IVs attached to both hands. Eddie and his parents had never felt so helpless. None of them could comfort her. She finally sobbed herself to sleep as her mother held her in her arms.

When she woke up the doctors came in and tested her as best as they could. Anna was indignant and withdrawn, not wanting to cooperate with anyone. They were told that the meningitis likely destroyed Anna's hearing, but they did not yet know how profound that loss was. She would need to be tested by an audiologist when she was released from the hospital. Now, as their parents stood talking to her doctors outside the room, Eddie sat beside Anna. She was so angry. So tense. How did he talk to his little sister? How did he find a way to get her to smile and laugh again, to tease and make fun of him they way only a sibling could? He didn't know anything about people who were deaf. How did they communicate? He would have to learn all of that. His whole family would.

Eddie reached for the notebook they were using to write questions from the doctors and nurses and try to explain what had happened to her. But how can you tell a sixteen year old that she would be deaf for the rest of her life?

You are not mute, Eddie wrote. *You can talk.* Then he handed the notebook to his sullen sister. She only glared at him.

Deaf is not dead, he continued. *You died...for thirty-nine seconds. That was how long it took for them to get your heart going again. You have always been stubborn.*

"I died?!" she said too loudly, looking at him incredulously.

Did you see a white light? What about Grandpa Monroe? Was he there? Grandma always said he was going to hell, so I would be surprised if you saw him hanging around. How about Bruno? Of course I'm not sure if dogs really go to heaven but I think that would be cool! He would make a really good guard dog for God at the pearly gates. Chase all those lesser deserving people away.

"You're not funny," she said.

Maybe you can get some really awesome hearing aids and tell people they are transmitters from Mars. I'll even make you a tin foil antenna hat like I had in second grade. Of course, I got punched in the face after school the day I wore that when I told Mikey Snodgrass he couldn't wear it because stupid boys like him could never be an astronaut.

The sadness in Anna's face was making him ache all over. How did he get her to see that she was full of life, and thankfully still had a long life ahead of her? He wouldn't tell her of the terror his parents and he had felt in the ER, waiting for the medical staff to save her but how could he make her feel grateful again for that life? Hell, she was a teenager. Her world was about school and boyfriends, music, dances and parties. It was not about death and illness and never hearing sound again. She had taken those things for granted, but now felt that all had been stolen from her.

You are the most stubborn person I have ever known. You would never take 'no' for an answer. Remember when you were eight years old and it was March and 35 degrees outside and you insisted on selling lemonade at the end of our driveway? None of us could talk you out of it. You sat out there for hours even when Mom kept trying to get you to come inside or sell hot cocoa instead. The lemonade finally froze and you crossed out "Lemonade .10" and wrote "Frozen Lemon Ice .15" and sold them all? You know how to take something that is not working or difficult and find another way. You are going to take that orneriness you got from Grandpa Monroe and figure out how to handle all this, and do it well. Hell, do it great.

As Anna read all this, her face slowly crumpled. The tears that flowed down her cheeks gathered at the neck of her hospital gown.

"It's not supposed to be like this, Eddie!" she said tearfully. "How do I live this way? All my friends are living the life I had just days ago. They're all going to desert me! I lost my music, my piano playing, even talking on the phone and watching television. I can't even communicate with my own family! How do I stop being scared of this silence?"

Eddie held his baby sister as she sobbed. Had she truly lost herself as well? Would she ever be that strong, stubborn girl again like the one that had tried selling frozen lemonade for hours in freezing weather? Deafness was so big, so life altering. Whatever it took, he vowed, he would help her to achieve it. But, she had to want to do this herself.

You embrace it he wrote to her and then wiped her face and nose with tissue and hugged her close. Anna's tears subsided to sniffles and occasional sobs. Even Eddie got lost in the silence that followed. For Eddie, it was a comfortable one. He was so grateful she had lived.

"Did you know Mikey Snodgrass is in law school?" Anna asked Eddie tentatively after they had sat there for a while.

Really? I told you he wasn't smart enough to be an astronaut, he wrote. Finally, the slightest glimpse of a smile from Anna as she read this. Eddie breathed a deep sigh. She would find that strength within herself. She would embrace her new life as best as she could. He would watch her grow to be a person she was always meant to be, a headstrong and confident woman.

***

In the police garage, Eddie took out his cell phone and clicked onto his contact list. It was time to make the call he was dreading ever since he had first realized his sister was missing. Not just missing, but vanished. How would he tell his niece Allyson that her mother had disappeared...disappeared right in the middle of a car accident?

CHAPTER FOUR

Allyson Anderson was ready for winter break, she thought, as she walked across the saturated grass and fallen leaves on the campus grounds of Indiana Mid-western University. The freezing rain mixed with snow had been coming down all morning and afternoon. This particular semester was extremely difficult. She had just taken her last finals in chemistry, her toughest subject. The sleepless nights, cold pizza, pots of hot coffee and round the clock studying had hopefully paid off for a good passing grade. She really needed to do well in this class so she could finally graduate in January with a Bachelor of Science in Nursing. As she walked across campus, she opened her backpack to check her cell phone. She'd left it turned off in class. Allyson was surprised to see several messages from her Uncle Eddie. Although he called her perhaps once a week to see how she was doing and to secretly, she thought with a smile, check up on her, he rarely called several times in one day. She would have to call him back once she got a chance.

Today was her mother's 50th birthday. Her family had planned a birthday party for her tomorrow night. Allyson would make the thirty-minute drive to her Mom's house the next day, after stopping to pick up the specially made cake she'd ordered. She laughed to herself, thinking about the silly pink princess cake that she'd picked out, knowing her Mom would get the joke. Her Dad Andy had always called Anna his Princess, Allyson had always giggled at this because her Mom hated girly-girl things and "boring" princess fairy tales. Every time she told one to Allyson she would change it to make the princesses modern and self-sufficient. There were no "happily ever after" endings, and all the modern Princesses ended up becoming corporate CEO's or real estate tycoons.

Allyson took out her red knitted hat and covered her dark blonde hair with it. It was so cold now that she could see the fog of her breath as she walked hurriedly across the campus grounds. The university was the same one where her parents had met at so many years before. She used to visit it often as a little girl, playing on the grass or running through the fallen leaves as she walked the grounds with her parents.

People were milling about, coming and going from classes, chattering excitedly about Christmas and leaving for home, or bemoaning the finals they needed to pass. Allyson waved at a few friends as she walked quickly across the street towards the older three-story house where she had a third floor room. The house was from the Victorian era, with a big wraparound porch and gingerbread trim. Its white paint and green shutters were faded and weathered, the porch stairs slightly askew and sinking into the ground. She was definitely a faded grand lady but Allyson loved the old house. She lived there for the past two years and felt lucky to find a place so close to the school. She even got used to climbing the three flights of stairs and having no air conditioning. Living on the top floor in summer's sweltering heat was quite the challenge, but Allyson worked days during the summer months at the University hospital and found ways to endure it when she had to. As she walked up to the steps of the front porch she saw to her surprise that her Uncle Eddie was standing by the front door. He turned at her approach and the love and concern on his face caused Allyson to stop in her tracks. Something was not right.

"What is it?" she asked him quietly. Eddie watched his niece's face, her cheeks were red from the cold and wind. She stood there staring at him with her blue-green eyes, her hands in their brown mittens clasped together. She was so much like her mother both in looks and temperament. She pulled off her mittens and clutched them to her chest, as her hair blew around her face. Eddie was instantly reminded of a day more than three years ago when he'd held her hand at her father Andy's funeral. It had been a cold day in November. There had been light rain then, a gloomy overcast sky. She had taken off her mittens so she could take one of the red roses from her father's casket at the grave site. He remembered how pale her face had been. It was devoid of tears, but her bruised, red rimmed, eyes showing the grief she had endured during the last year of her father's illness.

"Let's go inside," he said as he held out his hand to her. She searched his face for a long moment and took his hand. They slowly walked up the three flights of stairs, their footfalls echoing loudly throughout the home. Eddie, his breath coming in rapid gasps as he neared the top of the house, was tempted to joke about being too old and out of shape to climb all those stairs. He wanted to talk about anything but what he'd come there to tell her.

Allyson took out her key chain from her front pocket and unlocked the door to her small apartment. The two of them walked inside and Eddie closed the door behind them. He took in the limited space; the living room was also the bedroom, so there was a twin bed and a love seat, a dining table with just two chairs. The tiny kitchen was under an alcove just around the corner from the front door. It held a refrigerator, a microwave oven and a sink. There were a few cupboards above the sink painted in a cheerful yellow. The big A-shaped window was the focal point of the small room. Through it he could see the bare maple trees that lined the sidewalk in front of the old house. Their leaves were fallen now and the branches wet with rain. An ancient heater in one corner made a cranky, blustering noise as it gave heat to the cramped room. It could not stop the chill and numbness he had felt in the four hours that had passed since he had discovered his sister was missing.

"Tell me," Allyson said.

Eddie turned to look at her. She was sitting on the edge of her bed, her dark coat still on. Her backpack was on the floor where she'd tossed it. Eddie walked slowly to the loveseat and sat down heavily. He sighed. How the hell did he explain this?

"My Mom is fine. Everything is *fine*," she said almost angrily, as though daring him to contradict her. Her eyes were the color of a stormy sea. Anna had nick-named her "Stormy" as a teenager and she'd certainly lived up to that name during that tumultuous time of life. Her clutched hands and white knuckles betrayed her inner turmoil. She didn't really believe everything was fine. She knew he wouldn't be here if it was.

"I don't even know how to explain this, Allyson. I feel like I'm still asleep you know? Still waiting to wake up and start the whole day over," he took a deep breath and reached out and held her hands. "Your Mom is missing. The only way I can tell this is to start at the beginning."

He told her all of it from the start. How Jane picked up Anna at the library, how they had driven through the rain and sleet to Anna's favorite restaurant for lunch. He told her about the accident on Main street involving Jane's red sedan and the black SUV. He told her what the witnesses told him and he told her about being with Jane at the hospital, where he realized her mother was missing. He told her about going to the scene of the accident and questioning people and then to the police garage. He explained how he'd examined the car and found her mother's purse in the passenger seat. Allyson sat stoically throughout his story, shaking her head as she listened.

"I don't know where your Mom is, Allyson," he said softly. "It's like she just vanished into thin air. She disappeared in the middle of a car accident. I can't explain it better than that."

He expected some reaction from her. He expected she'd be frightened and anxious, maybe even cry. However, he was not prepared for the reaction she actually gave him.

She laughed. Not just laughed, but threw back her head and laughed uproariously. His surprised expression made her laugh harder, until tears came to her eyes and she had to clutch her chest.

"It's a joke right? Some kind of birthday prank," she said with a laugh as she wiped her wet eyes. "I know how the two of you love to play these jokes on each other and I have to admit, this one is *so* good! OK, I'll play along. So, what happens now? Do we go look for my Mom along the highway? Maybe we'll find her in a genie's bottle! I know! She's off fighting pirates and challenging Medusa for Poseidon's heart!"

Eddie looked at her for a long moment, then slowly took out a large envelope from under his coat jacket. He opened it and laid its contents beside Allyson on her bed. They were pictures of Jane's red car at the intersection after it had been hit by the SUV. The crumpled passenger side. The picture taken in the police garage of his wife's vehicle afterwards.

Allyson looked at them slowly, one by one. Finally, she picked up the first picture again, the one that showed the impact of the accident.

"No one could have lived through that," she whispered. Her face betrayed a wide range of emotions, but she kept shaking her head in denial.

Eddie handed his niece a picture of the black purse with the signature 'A' silver buckle on the front.

"This was found on the floor of the passenger seat."

Allyson took it slowly from him. Her father had given the purse to her mom years before. The running joke in their family had always been about the three of them having names that started with this letter. Her Dad had insisted that when Allyson was born her name had to start that way. *"She has to be of the A+ Team,"* he had joked to her mom. Not only did Allyson's name start with 'A,' but her middle name was also Anne. *"Your Dad just went 'A' little crazy,"* her Mom used to say.

She sat there for a moment holding tightly to the picture as she tried to make sense of what her Uncle Eddie was trying to tell here. There had to be some plausible explanation.

"Aunt Jane must have dropped her off somewhere! A store or

something. Or maybe she's even at home. I'm calling her now!"Allyson jumped up to get her cell phone out of her backpack. Eddie watched her, knowing she needed to do these things. She needed to draw her own conclusions. He watched as she dialed the number to her Mother's cell phone. Anna could talk back and forth to callers with the help of an online captioning service. She dialed the number over and over, getting frustrated each time as she waited and waited for a reply. She finally stopped trying.

"Let's go to the house now, Uncle Eddie. She must be there!"

She tossed her textbooks out of her backpack onto the floor and began shoving clothes into it. She smashed her hat back onto her head and grabbed her brown mittens.

Eddie picked up the photos and placed them back into the envelope. He followed his niece out the door and down the stairs. Allyson was rushing this time, almost stumbling down the old stairs. Eddie didn't blame her for this frenzied reaction. He had been so disbelieving and frantic himself and still felt like he was in some kind of mental fog. The two of them got into his Jeep and Eddie prepared to make the trip back to his sister's house.

During the thirty-minute drive neither of them said a word. Allyson didn't even glance his way. It was if looking at his worried face would make it all the more real. The rain had given way to snow and ice and she stared out the passenger side window, watching the white flurries that were now coming down heavily. Eddie concentrated on his driving. It was rush hour outside Indianapolis and it took all of his efforts to keep his jeep from plowing into some over-anxious suburbanite who couldn't wait for a green light so they could get out of the crowded city traffic. Eventually, the interstate gave way to the highway and to two-lanes and back roads through the farm lands that led to Greenway. It was dark now and the street lights had come on, illuminating the whiteness of the falling snow. Finally, he made the turn onto the street where his sister lived. The snow on the driveway outside Anna's Colonial style home was untouched. The tracks he himself had left hours before were now covered up.

Allyson jumped out of the passenger door as soon as he came to a stop. He watched her use her house key and open the front door, rushing inside and turning on lights. Eddie followed her inside and saw his niece running up the stairs. He heard her calling "Mom! Mom!" as her footsteps thudded across the floorboards upstairs, moving from room to room. He had already searched the whole house, top to bottom, himself.

Eddie turned on the light in the den. A Christmas tree was set up there. He walked slowly toward the tree and straightened the angel at the top. Glancing around the room he noticed the Anderson family photograph that hung on the wall opposite the tree. The three of them looked incredibly happy as they posed in front of a Christmas tree. Allyson was about five years old in the picture, wearing a velvet red dress and white tights with black shoes, grinning mischievously with her gap-toothed little girl smile. Andy was dressed in his dark suit and looked healthy and full of life. A much younger Anna was stunning in a black dinner dress. Her blonde hair framed her lovely face. He stood back and closed his eyes against the tears he wanted to shed. Not now.

"Mom! Mom!" Allyson continued shouting as she came running down the stairs.

Eddie watched as she ran through the dining room to the kitchen again. He could still hear her yelling. She came back to where Eddie stood in the den by the tree.

She stood there clutching her mittens again, this time in a stranglehold. "Why the hell am I yelling?" she said, "What is wrong with me? My mom is deaf!" Eddie put his arms around her and held her tight.

"Oh my God, Uncle Eddie! I'm so scared," she cried as she hugged him tight and the tears came. "I need to go look for her! She has to be somewhere!"

"I promise you I am doing everything I can to find her," he said. "My officers are out looking for her. We're searching the whole town. As soon as I learn anything, I'll tell you immediately. But for now, please come home with me and I'll take you to see Jane in the morning and do whatever it is you need to do."

"No!" she said and pulled away from him. "I need to be here! What if she comes back and she's hurt or...something," she cried out, her voice trailing off.

"I'll have an officer watch the house. He'll park right in the driveway. I don't think you should stay here alone, sweetheart." He reached out and touched her wet cheeks.

"I need to be here," she said, looking at him imploringly.

He hated leaving her alone but could tell by her stubborn stance that this would be a battle. She had already made up her mind.

"The whole thing is unreal!" she sobbed as he held her.

"I don't understand it either, Stormy...but I will," he said. "I promise that I will find out where your mom is. I promise you this."

CHAPTER FIVE

The lights on the family Christmas tree sparkled in the darkened room. Allyson lay on the couch, wrapped tightly in a warm afghan that had once belonged to her Grandma Monroe, as if it could protect her from the dark thoughts of despair that hovered in the air. The room caused a flood of mixed memories for her. It was a place where they'd laughed and played games, opened Christmas presents, watched television shows and grew as a family. The room where she had sneaked her first kiss when she was twelve years old with Pete Marshall on the very same couch where she now lay. The thread-worn couch should have been thrown out years before, but her mother never could find the heart to let it go because it wasn't just an insignificant object, but part of their family history. The happy times in this room were tarnished by one fairly recent memory. Her father Andy had used this room when he came home from the hospital, dying of renal cell cancer. Her strong, handsome father had become gaunt and aged, his face jaundiced and green eyes sunken. He had fought the battle to survive for more than two years and had finally come home to die.

Allyson squeezed her eyes tightly shut, trying to block out the pain of that memory. She desperately pushed those thoughts down. The family photograph of the three of them reminded her of a happier time. Grandpa Monroe had taken the photograph when she was just a little girl. She remembered that day vividly. They all had just decorated the tree and she was beside herself with eagerness for the coming Christmas, chattering excitedly about Santa and the gifts she was hopeful to get.

She recalled the conversation she had had with her father in that room as she sat on his lap on this very couch wearing her new Christmas dress. She had demanded that he tell her the story, yet again, of how he and her mother had met.

"Please, Daddy!" she said.

"OK, OK," her father said with a smile on his face. He looked at her mother and she shook her head at them, knowing he would give in. This was his story to tell.

"Princess Anna and I met in college," he said out loud as his hands signed the words. Her mother was watching them with a gentle smile on her face.

"The first time I saw her, I fell to my knees in astonishment at her beauty." He had literally fallen to his knees when he had met her but he did not tell his five year old daughter that it was because he'd actually tripped over a tree root and fallen headfirst into her as she sat on the ground outside, studying. He also didn't say that her beautiful mother had angrily yelled as he detangled himself from her lap, "Get the hell off me!"

"Her beauty left me speechless. I could not find the words to say to her what was in my heart. I stood there trembling like a tree in the forest. How could I, a mere common man, win the love of this fair princess?" Allyson's eyes grew round and she covered her mouth and giggled. Her parents glanced at each other and tried not to laugh.

"Alas, she walked away from me that day, without a backwards glance. But, I knew that I had to follow her and plead with her, beg if I must. I needed her to understand that my intentions were pure and that I was the man she was meant to be with."

He didn't tell her that he watched her mother from afar, noticing how she kept to herself, and her soft, careful speech as she talked to her professor. It was then that he had realized that she was deaf. She was also angry. Every time he tried to talk to her, she had brushed past him and said "go away". Andy had learned sign language in high school. His father had been a Baptist minister and a few people from their small church community had been deaf. Andy took it upon himself to ask them to teach him so that he could sign his father's sermons for them every Sunday.

He tried to sign to her one day and thought she would slap his face. "Do you think I'm stupid? I know how to talk perfectly well," she had said, her stance defensive. The wall she had put up since she was sixteen years old was now insurmountable.

"The Princess lived in a beautiful white castle. It was surrounded by stone walls. I tried and I tried, but I could not get past these walls. They were too high to climb over and too hard to break. I was saddened with great despair that I might never win her heart," he said dejectedly. Allyson looked up at him with worry in her eyes. She had heard this story so many times, but each time she felt like it was the first time.

"Daddy! You have to, or I won't be bornt!" she said to him. He smiled down at her sweet face. She was so much like her mother.

"As sad as I was, I would never give up! I was a clever young man. I would find a way in! I tried one thing after another."

"I tried singing a beautiful song to her."

He had sung "Bridge Over Troubled Waters"...badly, hoping with her deafness that the screeching tone of his voice wouldn't make any difference anyway. She had looked at him in cold disdain as he made a fool of himself, dancing and singing in a circle around her, acting out the words to the song with great flourish.

"I tried launching myself over the castle wall."

He had literally fallen down a short flight of stairs one day in the main hall as he had tried to get her attention as she walked up the other side. Only his pride had been bruised but she had glanced at him in concern and started to walk towards him. He smiled at her sheepishly as she neared. When she realized he was fine, he heard her curse under her breath. Yet, as he watched her walk away, he saw a small smile on her face. Finally.

"I tried beating up the ugly, smelly ogres who roamed outside the castle. I would not let them get near my Princess! No matter how big they were or how mean, I would protect her!"

He had gotten a crazy idea after falling down the stairs. He had asked one of the football players to punch him in the face. Not too hard, mind you. The football player had been happy to help. Too happy. Andy had known Anna's schedule very well by then and he had acted out an "argument" with the football player one day as she was passing by. The football player had hauled off and punched him right in the nose. He hadn't expected his nose to break, but, it did. He hadn't expected the gush of blood to spurt through the air and all over his face either. He remembered the shock on the player's face as he sat woozily on the ground, trying to clear his head. He heard the player apologizing and most of all he had heard Anna's sweet voice rising in anger as she cursed at this guy. The football player had tried to help him up but Anna had kicked him in the leg and told him to get lost. She'd helped Andy to the infirmary and even driven him to the hospital so they could reset his nose. He'd looked at her goofily with adoring eyes the whole time, even when he'd thrown up in her car. After she had helped him back to his dorm room, he told her the truth. Of course he was on heavy medication then which certainly contributed to his honesty. She'd been speechless. She stood there just gaping at him. "I just want to get to know you," he said forlornly as he stood there with his broken nose and puffy face. Actually, it had come out slightly more slurred than that. He wasn't sure at first if she'd read his lips. She must have sensed the sincerity coming from him, or hell, maybe she felt sorry for him. Either way, she had surprised him by shyly saying "OK"

"One day, I got a brilliant idea. I would find a dragon and tame him. The dragon would let me hold onto him and fly me over the castle walls! But, where could I find a dragon? I looked and I looked! I climbed mountains and swam oceans! I got lost in the woods while I was searching one day and a fairy told me of a very special dragon

that lived in a cave close by," he said. *"I walked all night and the next morning I came upon this cave and right inside it waiting was a very large...pink dragon! The dragon was not a "him" at all, it was a girl! The dragon saw me and almost set me on fire. Luckily, I had my shield and sword and protected myself!"*

They had dated and gotten to know each other. Anna had finally begun to trust him. Best of all was the sex. A man should always have sex with an angry girl.

"The dragon looked at me a long time and saw the goodness in my heart. I climbed up on the dragon and she flew me over the woods and mountains and oceans, right to the castle wall where the princess lived. The dragon let me down on the grass inside the courtyard, right next to my beautiful princess. I waved goodbye at the dragon as she flew away."

Five year old Allyson could hardly contain herself, picturing in her mind the wonderful story.

"I got down on my knees besides her and told her how much I loved her, how much I admired her strength and courage. I told her that I would love her for the rest of my life. That I would fight any battle for her and stand beside her when life got hard and times were dark. I held her hand and asked her to marry me. She looked at me for a long time."

"What did she say?" Allyson demanded at the long pause. Andy looked at her mother sitting across from them, remembering the night he had proposed. It happened after they had been dating almost three years. He had been teaching her sign language after she had asked him to. At first, she was very tentative but had gotten better with practice. He had been using index cards with pictures of the sign and words to teach her. She had read then signed each one for him. The last three cards he held had been MARRIAGE ME YOU.

Anna looked at him, and signed, "yes" across the room to him, just as she had ten years before.

"She said she would love me forever and that she wanted nothing more than to be my princess." Allyson clapped her hands with glee

and hugged him close. She was so happy to be surrounded by her loving parents and grandparents. It was one of the best Christmases ever.

Now she sat in the same room where all this happened so many years ago, alone in the dark. Both her grandparents were gone now and so was her father. Her beloved Daddy. So full of honesty and courage and laughter. After he died, she rarely came home. There was a huge gulf in their family unit now. The brightest light in it had gone out. At first, Allyson and her mother called each other often on the captioned phone. At times, they struggled about what to say. The connection they now had was centered on memories of sadness and loss and instead of leaning on each other they moved apart. When they were together these last three years everything seemed forced and strained. They shared those moments of taking care of her father, the moments of his pain and great suffering. His tears and helplessness. They shared the hopelessness together when he finally gave up the fight. It was something neither of them wanted to think about any longer, so, they pretended to be fine.

Allyson closed her eyes and let the tears flow. She and her mother had both focused so much on what they had lost, that they had almost forgotten what they still had in front of them. Her mother was missing in some bizarre, unexplainable way. How could it be? It took everything she had not to run screaming out the door. To just run through the cold and snow, calling out her mother's name over and over. Was it crazy to think that while her mother might not be able to hear her calling for her, she still would have felt it in her soul? Allyson buried her face in her grandmother's afghan and sobbed. She whispered a prayer that her mother would feel all the love she had for her from wherever she was. Feel it and let it bring her home.

CHAPTER SIX

Jane Monroe lay in her hospital bed sleeping. She looked like she had been in a fist fight and lost, badly. The hospital had wanted to keep her overnight for observation. She still had a slight concussion. Her broken nose was set and bandaged but she might need the skills of a plastic surgeon to fix it just the way it was before. Eddie told her that it gave her face character, but he smiled sadly as he said it, his eyes roaming over her fine, delicate features. Jane and Eddie had first started dating their senior year in high school, although they attended different schools, he in Greenway, and Jane in Indianapolis. He had visited a local floral shop to buy his mother Maria, flowers for her birthday and Jane was working there part time because she wanted to obtain a degree in biochemistry when she went to college at Purdue the following fall. It was the same shop that she would later buy and still owned. Eddie was taken with her porcelain-like beauty, her long dark hair and wide brown eyes. She was so petite that she barely came up to his shoulder. Now more than 30 years later, she was much older, but still so beautiful to him. Her dark hair was sprinkled with gray now and cut short, and her face showed delicate lines around her eyes and mouth. The two of them were still so much in love with each other that they knew the others' feelings without having to say a word.

Eddie and Jane only talked a few minutes about his trip to get Allyson and how she was doing when he'd come back to her room late that night. They talked about the search for Anna and all that was being done to find her. Jane could sense his turmoil and apprehension and she tried to hide her own. Where was Anna? Jane's heart pounded in fearful dread every time she thought of her. None of it was possible, but still, it happened just the same. She had gone over every second of her time with Anna in the car, but her head had hurt painfully after so much mental searching.

She knew the times in their marriage when he just needed her silence, to trust in him and just to believe in him. As much as she wanted to keep questioning him, she knew that he'd already explained to her everything he knew. She had fallen asleep holding tightly to his hand.

Jane dreamed that she was sitting inside her red car. The car was stopped in the middle of a two-lane road that ran through the cornfields outside town. She glanced around the interior of the car and saw that she was totally alone. The air outside her sedan was thick with fog. There were no sign of any other vehicles on the road. No sign of any life at all but hers. She looked at the passenger seat and felt dread building inside her.

"Anna!" she shouted, "Where are you?"

Her breathing quickened and came in small gasps. Jane opened the car door and got out. She couldn't see more than ten feet in front of her. The air was so oppressive that she had to take deep breaths to calm herself to keep from passing out.

"Anna!"

All of a sudden she heard her name being called as from a great distance.

"Anna! Where are you?" Jane yelled as she searched the area for her sister-in-law. She could see what looked like corn stalks lining the road, their silhouettes dark and ominous. Jane felt her heart thudding in fear. She started walking away from the car towards where she had heard her name being called, looking back to keep an eye on the

vehicle. She did not want to get lost in this obscuring mist.

"Anna!" she called again and for some reason her legs would no longer move forward. Suddenly, she spotted Anna in the distance on the highway, shrouded in fog. Jane felt such a wave of relief that it almost brought her to her knees with gratitude. Anna was dressed in the same clothes she had been wearing when Jane had picked her up from work that afternoon. She looked frightened and confused.

"Where am I? Jane, where am I?" Anna said with a voice full of terror. Jane tried to walk toward her but the fog seemed to be clinging to her now, as if holding onto her with invisible vines. Anna started to cry and Jane noticed she seemed to be fading away.

"No, Anna! Come back!" she called.

Anna looked at Jane sadly. "I'm dead, Jane. Can't you feel it?"

"No, Anna! You are not dead! Walk toward me!"

She looked at Jane one last time and with great sorrow in her voice said "I'm dead, Jane," and disappeared altogether.

"No, no, no! Anna! Anna!" Jane screamed into the fog that was now closing over her. "Not dead! You are not dead!"

Jane awoke from her dream with a violent start, gasping for air and clutching the bed sheets.

"Not dead," she whispered.

***

The evidence from the accident sat in a box on Eddie's desk in his small office cubicle. He pulled out the envelope and looked again at the photocopies taken by witnesses on their cell phones. For what felt like the hundredth time, he read the statements made by passersby and from those that had rushed to help. He'd studied everything over and over again in the last few hours. Richard Lowery, the slightly intoxicated man who had caused the accident, had been interviewed as well and he also could not recall how many people were in the car that he hit. Whether this lapse was caused by the amount of alcohol involved or real memory, they would never know. Conflicting the evidence also was that only those that were "sure" there were two women in the car had been more than a block from the accident. They were the ones who had witnessed the red sedan moving down Main Street towards the green light before it had been plowed into by the black SUV at the intersection.

Eddie picked up one of the photocopies taken of the impact of the accident. He could clearly see the date and time of day on the Bank marquee showing in the pictures background:

12-12-2012

12:12 pm

This time and date reference was on several of the photos taken. The police officer in him felt a prickle of unease running along the back of his neck. He was still missing something tangible, but it continued to elude him like how a fine mist covers a river just before dawn, the shadowy blanket making the water seem like a dark patch of ground, and obscuring what truly lay beneath. He picked up another photo, which had been taken right after the two vehicles had collided. His eyes ran slowly over each image, the damage to the sedan, his wife Jane slumped in the driver's seat with the airbag imploded over her face. The crumpled passenger side still yawning gray metal and leaking black oil, showing the vehicle's ribcage. He looked closer at the picture of the passenger side. The place his sister should have been sitting was empty and dark. At the very top of the smashed passenger door was a glint of white like a flashbulb had gone off. It was so small that Eddie passed it by many times without giving it a thought, but now he sat studying this spherical like image. Very curious indeed because it looked like it could have been a glint from the sun shining down on a luminous surface. But, that couldn't be. It was raining heavily at the time of the accident. Just a coincidence perhaps, but right now Eddie didn't believe in anything coincidental or even remotely normal. He rubbed his tired face.

Mark Browning came in the front door as Eddie was staring at the photograph. It was now after midnight. Anna had been missing for twelve hours and the two had been going non-stop since the accident.

He hadn't wanted to leave Allyson alone at his sister's house but she'd insisted that she would be fine. She wanted him to go back to work so he could find her mother.

Mark sat heavily at his desk in the corner, tossing an envelope on top of the mess that had been made during frantic phone calls and the pile-up of evidence paperwork. There were other volunteers in the outer office making phone calls and writing statements and making coffee. Everyone in the small town now knew that Anna was missing and many had volunteered to help any way they could. Eddie was very grateful for their compassion and caring and eagerness to help. Groups of volunteers had searched through the town for his sister; every store had been walked through and investigated. Almost every street and highway in the county had been scrutinized.

"Nothing about this is logical," he said to Mark as he walked over to his desk.

Mark stretched his neck and shoulders and sighed, then ran a hand through his messy hair and closed his eyes for a moment.

"OK, don't think I am crazy, boss, but maybe it's time to look at this illogically," he said.

"Illogically how?" asked Eddie.

"I don't know. Hell, I can't think. Look at it illogically like...a magician's trick," Mark said sheepishly.

As Eddie stared at him, all the frustration about his sisters disappearance that had been slowly boiling in his stomach, began to build into a full steaming kettle of anger.

"OK, I'll look at it illogically. I've got it!" Eddie said, letting his voice rise. Eddie never lost his temper in the office, and his words brought everyone to a startled halt, "The impact of the accident caused my sister to shrink to the size of a peanut!" he yelled. "Now she is 'this small'," gesturing something tiny with his thumb and forefinger, "and is right now lost in the police garage dodging car parts and giant rusty nails and humongous mice who want to eat her for dinner!"

Eddie ran to his desk and opened up a drawer. He flung papers left and right until he finally pulled something out from underneath a file. He strode back to Mark's desk and tossed it on the mess. It was a magnifying glass.

"Take this," he said, "go to the garage, go over every square centimeter of that car, and don't come back until you find my sister, or you're fired!"

He stood there breathing heavily, glaring at Mark who had become red in the face and stood there staring back at him with hurt in eyes. Eddie knew he'd finally lost it. He glanced around at the concerned faces of the people in the office. Every single one of them cared about him and his family. They'd always been there for each other, to comfort them in times of sorrow and loss. He raked his fingers jerkily through his hair.

"Sorry," he whispered to Mark, and turned, walked fast to the restroom and closed the door. In the mirror, his eyes were filled with worry and tension. He closed them and took several deep breaths then splashed cold water on his face and neck. He stood there for a few minutes just letting the numbness overtake him again, them he dried his face and muttered "*Get a grip!*" He didn't look at anyone as he walked back to his desk and sat in his chair.

Mark walked slowly over to his boss desk. He looked at him with embarrassment and sympathy but he knew that under the circumstances it might be best that Eddie got this anger out now. He felt little hope that any of this would end well. It was the craziest thing he had ever been a part of.

"Chief, I think you should take a look at the memory card I pulled up from the Speedvision video recorder from the Main Street location," he told Eddie carefully.

Eddie got up tiredly from his chair and walked to Mark's desk with him. Mark typed a few words onto his keyboard and brought up the digital recording of the traffic from the day before onto his computer. Eddie leaned over Mark's shoulder and looked at the camera view of the vehicles driving by. They'd had to install the camera a few months ago because road construction in the county had caused most traffic to be detoured right through town.

At 12:11:36 pm he spotted his wife's red sedan at the stop light on Main and Washington Avenue, two blocks before the accident had taken place. Even though it was raining heavily, he could clearly see through the slightly tinted windows the inside of the red car and the outline of Jane's head and shoulders and facial features. He could tell she was talking to the person sitting in the passenger seat while she was driving. He looked closer and drew in his breath. It was Anna. Less than twenty-four *seconds* before the accident had occurred his sister was sitting in the passenger seat of his wife's car.

CHAPTER SEVEN

The media descended on the small town of Greenway, Indiana with a vengeance. The story of the disappearing woman had first gone out over the airwaves two days before. Eddie had given a very brief statement at that time to the local media, but the world had gotten a hold of this curious and strange occurrence. How could someone disappear in the middle of a car accident?

The media came in droves to the farm community outside of Indianapolis. Trucks and cars carrying eager reporters, vans with television station logos printed in large letters on the side arrived along with crews and cameramen lugging heavy audio and video equipment. The tiny town filled up quickly. Every parking space was taken. Even the local churches and grocery parking lots were filled. Eddie drove slowly through a sea of people to get to his parking space at the police station the next morning. As he got out of his Jeep, a swarm of reporters had pounced on him.

"Chief Monroe, I understand that the missing woman is your sister Anna Anderson. Have you been able to find her at all?" one said, scrambling to his side.

"Chief, can you tell us again what happened?" said another as she thrust a microphone in his face. Eddie offered a terse "No comment," as he tried in vain to push through the media onslaught.

"Chief Monroe, do you think your sister is dead?" a man wearing a black suit and red tie asked him as he headed for the side door. Eddie looked at him incredulously.

"No, I don't think that! There is no physical evidence to support such a statement!" he spat back at the reporter, his anger rising. "I'll be giving an official statement in a few hours. I ask that all of you remember that this is a small, tight-knit community. Please be respectful of our citizens and our town."

Mark Browning pushed his way through the crowd and helped guide Eddie to the side door of the office building. He locked the door after them. "The FBI is on the phone," he said. "They want to discuss the accident and Anna's disappearance."

Shit. Just what I needed, Eddie thought and groaned out loud.

"Call Sheriff Cole and the State Police and see if they will send some help to control these crowds," he told Mark. The city of Greenway had two other full time police officers and four part time ones. They were all out working that morning on various calls mostly concerning the amount of disorder the news media and their vehicles had caused. It seemed like every citizen in town was complaining.

Eddie entered his office and hung his coat up. He shook his head at the crowd out the window. What a circus. And then he sat down at his desk and picked up the phone to talk to the FBI agent on hold. Could this week get any worse?

***

The small brick Greenway Community Center was ablaze with light that evening. The building housed next to the city jail was used for various city and council meeting and the occasional fundraiser. News reporters and local citizens hurried through the cold and snow so they could get a seat inside.

Eddie stood at the front of the room next to the podium and surveyed the crowd. All the seats were taken and people were standing at the back of the room. State Police had sent four officers to help them out and he could see them in their dark blue shirts and blue uniform pants trying to bring some kind of orderly control over the crowd.

Yesterday, he had taken Allyson to the hospital with him to pick up Jane when she was released. The two women had held each other for a long time and cried. Allyson had questioned her over and over about the day her mother disappeared but Jane couldn't tell her anything more than she already knew. They drove Jane home and left her in the care of a close friend and Eddie took Allyson to the scene of the accident. She had gotten out of his car and stood staring at the street, trying to imagine it all in her head. He drove her to the library to talk to Anna's friends and co-workers and they told her the same things that they had told the police the day before. Allyson had finally told him to take her home and to go back to work. His heart ached at her sadness and helplessness.

That morning, he'd sent an officer to Anna's house to keep away the reporters that had descended in droves on her home and neighborhood as well. He hated leaving Allyson alone through so much of this. She would not persuaded to stay elsewhere. She told him when her mother returned, it would be to her home. There was never a question of "if" she returned, only when.

Jane remained at home, bedridden with constant headaches. She had been his rock throughout this whole ordeal. He knew how hard she had tried to push away her own fear and uncertainty about all of this craziness she was so much a part of. He was so thankful she understood his need to be doing everything and anything at all that would help him solve the puzzle of Anna's disappearance.

"We're here to help any way that we can Eddie," Sheriff Cole told him, shaking his hand. A big man in his early 60's, Sheriff James Cole had a balding head that gleamed under the lights and intelligent gray eyes that looked at him in sympathy. Eddie had seen him strong-arm gang members and disarm robbery suspects faster than one would expect for a man of his age and girth. He had a soft, kind voice and too many people had paid the price for mistaking that voice for weakness. Eddie had approached Sheriff Cole many times since Jane's accident for suggestions and advice. Their offices were working together, but unfortunately, there was just not a lot either of them could do that had not been already done.

"Thanks, Jim. I appreciate that more than you know," Eddie said.

"Can we please have some kind of quiet?" Mark Browning said into the microphone as he addressed the crowd. "Chief Monroe will be making his statement now."

Eddie stepped up to the podium. He glanced around the room at the media cameras, reporters and lights. He had never in his fifty-five years seen anything like this.

"My name is Edward Monroe," he said. "I am the Police Chief for the city of Greenway, Indiana. My office is in charge of the investigation that we are all here to discuss tonight. Please remember that this is an active, on-going investigation and that some things will not be made public at this time, if ever. I am going to go ahead and answer the obvious questions. I'll take a few questions from those of you who wish to ask anything further following my statement."

It was hot in the room. Eddie paused, took a deep breath, and began. He explained the circumstances of the accident, beginning with the timing, adding witness reports and concluding with Jane's trip to the emergency room and the discovery that Anna was missing. He also added that the driver of the black SUV, Richard Lowery, was given a field sobriety test and transported by police to the hospital for observation. He had a blood alcohol content level of 0.8% and was arrested for driving under the influence causing injury and transported to the city jail.

Eddie poured a glass of water from the carafe on the podium. He could feel rivulets of sweat running down his neck and back. He knew he was talking monotonously but he just wanted the whole thing to be over with. It took all his control to not give into the feelings of turmoil that sat in his belly. He discussed his interview with Jane to the crowd.

"Mrs. Monroe stated at the hospital that her sister-in-law, Mrs.

Anna Anderson, was a passenger in her car at the time of the accident. She stated that she picked her up in her car outside the Greenway Public Library at approximately 12 noon. Four co-workers of Mrs. Anderson's from the library would also make statements that Mrs. Anderson was seen getting into the passenger side of Mrs. Monroe's car outside at that time. Video surveillance of Main Street on December 12th, 2012 would show the red Miata being driven west at 12:11 pm and that the camera would show that two people were inside the vehicle at that time. Further review of the video would confirm that the passengers were these two women. As previously mentioned, all witnesses and first responders have stated that Mrs. Anderson was not present inside the vehicle at the scene of the accident which then occurred 24 seconds later."

Eddie continue on, describing finding Anna's purse in the police garage on the floorboard of the wrecked sedan and the search for her at her home and throughout the town. "An All-Points-Bulletin went out for her yesterday and she is officially listed as a missing person and we do not know her whereabouts at this time. I'll answer just a few questions now. Please just one question at a time."

The crowd clamored to be heard and Mark stepped up to call order again. "One at a time, please!" He pointed at a young woman at the front and said "Go ahead."

"Chief Monroe, Jennifer Nelson, WLFD Chicago. Can you confirm that Jane Monroe and Anna Anderson are your wife and sister?"

"Yes, that is fact."

"Is your sister Anna Anderson deaf, Chief Monroe?" another reporter yelled out to him.

"Yes she is."

"Do you wish to expand on that, chief?"

"No, I don't. It's irrelevant." Eddie said. God, Anna would have hated this line of questioning. He and Jane had watched the late news from Indianapolis last night and the lead story had been "Deaf Woman Disappears during Car Accident." They knew the statement would have inflamed Anna's ire.

"Chief Monroe, Brian Little, WKTV, Indianapolis," said a man at the front in a crisp blue suit. "You've been an officer for 18 years, is this correct? Can you tell us in your own words, from a professional standpoint, what you think happened here? What happened to your sister?"

Eddie looked around the room at the horde of people. He was reminded of the time he chased a perpetrator into an abandoned building outside town when he was a rookie police officer. He chased this guy from room to room and down a flight of stairs. As he entered what he assumed was the basement, he saw a swarm of rats bunched in one corner. They looked back at him, unafraid, as if he was the intruder, not them. He knew most of people in the room cared nothing at all about his missing sister. They probably didn't even care if she was ever found. They only cared about the story. He had to remind himself to not go all John Wayne and whip out his revolver and shoot off a few rounds at the ceiling just to make himself feel like he was still the one in charge.

"I have been a police officer for 18 years, yes," he said at last. "I can tell you that as a professional investigator, I look at both the facts of a case and the evidence. In this particular case the evidence contradicts the facts, i.e. the perceived truth. I do not have any doubt whatsoever that Mrs. Anderson was a passenger in this car on the day of the accident. I also can tell you there is no evidence other than the video surveillance and Mrs. Anderson's personal property on the floorboards that she was inside the vehicle at the *time* of this accident."

He wiped his forehead with the back of one hand. "You ask my professional opinion on what happened to my sister and I'll tell you that at this moment, I don't know the answer to that question. However, I will find that out. No matter how long it takes."

A reporter pushed to the front of the crowd, waving his mike. "Are you admitting that your sister, Anna Anderson disappeared into thin air, Chief Monroe?" he asked.

"I'm not admitting that," Eddie said. "At this time there will be no further questions. Thank you." He had had enough. Motioning to Mark that it was over, he stepped down from the podium as the crowd continued to scream questions. Mark and Sheriff Cole escorted Eddie to the back of the building and out to their waiting vehicles. Eddie drew in a shaky breath and closed his eyes as he sat in his Jeep. Somehow he would find out the answer to Anna's disappearance. Somehow.

CHAPTER EIGHT

It was now four days since Anna had disappeared. Eddie was exhausted by it all. Exhausted by not having any leads about his sister. Exhausted by being hounded by the media and trying to keep the peace in his small town while handling an investigation that seemed to have spiraled out of his control. The stress was taking a toll on him. He'd laid awake for hours, the night before, then gotten up before sunrise so not to waken Jane. She'd had nightmares almost every night since she had came home from the hospital. Listening to her cries and pleas for help as she tossed and turned on the bed made his heart hurt. He didn't know how to comfort her.

He went to see Allyson every day, bringing her groceries and case updates and a rundown of the day's events. She'd been surprisingly calm. Her belief that her mother would be found was unwavering.

As he waited for the sun to rise, he'd sought comfort in his dad's old recliner, a dark brown chair that had turned a milk chocolate hue after so many years of use. His mother Maria had gotten the chair for his dad almost 18 years ago. His mother had liked to quip that the chair had become part of his dad Bill's ass.

Eddie smiled at the reminiscence. His father had been a wonderful man. It really was a comfortable chair. He thought about his parents and a sad nostalgia engulfed him.

William "Bill" Monroe had been an Army Major and World War II veteran when he met Maria Anne Wyatt in 1946 while he was stationed at Fort Benjamin Harrison in Lawrence, Indiana. They both were 25 years old. Bill had already seen and done many things in his short life. He had been stationed in Poland during much of the war where he'd seen heavy combat and huge loss of life. When he came home all he could think about was finding some type of normalcy and starting his own family when his service was up. He hoped to buy a small farm where he could raise corn, soybeans and hay and try and forget the time of his life when it was filled with war and bloodshed. But he would never forget the men he had served with who never got to come home.

He'd met Maria at a benefit dance held off the base. She was the only child and heir of a third generation farmer and Bill asked to meet her father and talk to him about starting his own place one day. They'd quickly become fast friends and Maria had always joked that Bill and her father had fallen in love at first sight. Once they had married, Maria's father offered Bill a partnership in the farm.

Farming was a hard way of life but Bill loved working with his hands and the soil, planting crops and watching them grow, and nurturing them to fruition. Once the war had ended there was a great need to rebuild, grow crops and mass produce consumer goods. He had felt such accomplishment from being able to provide a living and take care of his family. Some years were better than the next, but it was a good life.

Maria and Bill wanted to start a family right away but it had taken several miscarriages and almost ten years before Eddie was born. His parents had pretty much given up hope in having children and his coming had been met with surprise and gratitude. Anna being born five years later when they were both in their early 40's was another shock, but still such a blessing to them.

Anna and Eddie never wanted for love or affection, or something to do. They helped plant seed and harvest produce, took care of the chickens their Mom raised, learned to drive the tractor and picked and sold berries that grew wild on their farm. The farm was close to 300 acres and was barb-wire fenced around the perimeter because their Grandfather Wyatt used to breed cattle before the war. Bill had not kept cattle for beef production but did maintain some dairy cows for their own use, he preferred to concentrate on the planting of hay, soybeans and corn for cash crop.

Unfortunately, Eddie never wanted to be a full time farmer. When his parents had gotten on in age they'd come to town and lived with him and Jane. The old house was no longer used except for an occasional retreat. They'd hired help to continue to farm a small amount of corn and soybeans on the property, but almost all the money from selling their produce went for property taxes, insurance, seed and upkeep.

His Mom had passed away in 2002 and his dad followed just eight months later. All the life and energy and happiness seemed to have left Bill when his beloved wife had passed away. He seemed broken and empty, as if just passing time until he could join her. Eddie could understand, as he didn't know how he himself could live a full life without Jane. He was almost glad his parents weren't alive to experience this heartache over Anna's disappearance.

He got up from his dad's chair and rubbed his own ever-widening ass, smiling a little as he thought of his mother's comment. He drew the curtain back and looked out the window. More snow was coming down. It was still officially fall, yet but it already seemed like the longest winter of his life. He had been a police officer for so long now, and felt incredible weariness when he thought of his job, not just from his sister's disappearance, but from the stress of the job itself. It might not have been the kind of stress that a big city police officer would have, but it was stressful just the same. He felt old.

He closed his tired eyes and thought about riding a tractor and the smell of freshly turned dirt and the feeling of accomplishment when the planting was done or crops had been gathered. Maybe one day he would do what generations of his family had done for over 150 years.

He opened his eyes and let the window curtain drop. Oh hell, who was he kidding. Farming was a tough life. He remembered years when their family struggled to make ends meet. Some years the toll and stress added more lines of weariness to his parents faces. But at least there was always plenty of good healthy food on their table no matter the hard times.

Still, maybe it was time to let go of the stress and start anew. Find renewal like the coming of spring. He needed something to thaw the bitter chill of Anna's disappearance which sat on his heart like a block of ice.

***

Jane Monroe lay staring into the blackness of her bedroom. She'd known the moment when Eddie had gotten up from his restlessness, even though he'd risen as quietly as he could so as not to disturb her. She felt his helplessness and fear over Anna's disappearance as if it were her own. In most ways, it was her own pain as well.

She went over and over the circumstances of December 12th. She could remember certain things clearly, like how Anna looked that day. Her dark blonde hair fell just below her shoulders. She had worn her black jacket with fur trimmed hood. She had on a dark blue cable-knit sweater underneath her coat and had worn black dress slacks. She could remember Anna smiling at her as she sat there in her car, but the rest of the events that took place, picking her up from the library, making the short drive toward the restaurant to have lunch and the accident was starting to become a shrouded memory.

Jane remembered the first time she had met Anna more than 30 years before. Her first impression of Anna was that she was careful about who she included in her circle of self-preservation and trust. Eddie already told her about Anna's illness as a teenager and loss of hearing. She still seemed very defensive about her abilities to overcome any challenge that her deafness brought out in her life.

Anna had been dating Andy about three years at that time and they were teaching the rest of the Monroe family sign language. Jane watched the way they had all interacted and laughed with each other and felt their closeness and love as a family. Eddie and Bill had a tough time signing with their thick fingers, but they tried hard to learn it just the same. Anna was so good at lip-reading that sometimes Jane wondered why she needed to learn sign language at all. It seemed that her family and Andy only used it when Anna couldn't understand what was being said to her. She very rarely used it herself to communicate.

Jane remembered a conversation they'd had while shopping for her wedding a few months later.

"Your lip-reading is so good, Anna, why did you feel the need to learn sign language?" she asked her while struggling to fit her size 8 foot into a six 6 1/2 white satin slipper to go with the dress she had picked out.

"At first, I never even considered it." Anna said, as she pulled on blue satin high-heeled bridesmaid slippers. "I looked at it as something that would make me different, make me stand out. I didn't want to be noticed, to bring attention to myself. It would have been like having "Deaf" tattooed on my forehead." She admired the shoe in the glass partition, then tried to walk and stumbled. She sat down with a laugh and looked up at Jane.

"I wasn't open to learning until after I met Andy," she said, tugging the shoes off. "He told me that if I wanted to learn he would teach me, and he never brought it up again until I asked him. I was starting to see for myself how difficult lip-reading could be. I could read my family pretty well, but strangers were a whole different situation. I struggled to understand my teachers and even the friends I had known for years. Conversations became short and frustrating. I can communicate verbally pretty well but I found myself just shaking my head yes or no a lot and getting odd looks from people who asked me questions that I didn't understand."

She dropped the slippers back in the shoe box, and put it down. "There were so many times when I lip-read people totally wrong," Anna continued. "Do you know how tough it was to understand a college math professor discussing the difference in linear and exponential functions to logarithmic and polynomial characteristics? I know that using sign language in these situations probably wouldn't have mattered but I started to realize that I needed another way to communicate too. It's like having a second language I guess. Plus, Andy is teaching me. I always tell him that looking at his mouth makes me way too hot and flustered to lip-read him well, so I'd better learn to sign."

She smiled at Jane then, just as she had that day she'd gotten in her car just a few days ago. So full of life.

Jane thought again of Andy and Anna her wedding. The two of them were so beautiful together. Andy so handsome with his dark hair and green eyes, so protective of this young woman he was so obviously in love with. Some people are just meant to be together and that these two found each other was in itself a kind of miracle.

She lay there in the darkness, listening to Eddie walk about the house. His pacing beat out a lonely rhythm across the house's wooden floors. She wished she could tell him exactly what happened to his sister while she was in her car. She clenched her hands in frustration as she tried to remember the accident. Was the ever-present headache meant to be a reminder of that day or was it there to protect her from digging too deep inside herself? Perhaps the truth about Anna's disappearance was more painful than any of them could ever handle.

CHAPTER NINE

Allyson stared out the kitchen window at the mob of ever present reporters. The State and Greenway police cars drove by often trying to clear the street and her Uncle Eddie had assigned an officer to be present in front of her house at all times, but they couldn't make them go away.

Kindly neighbors brought casserole dishes of food for her and handed them to the officer on duty. But she didn't let them in. She didn't want to talk to anyone about her mother's disappearance. Her friends from college had called over and over, but she finally started glancing at the call numbers and letting most go to voicemail. Uncle Eddie and Aunt Jane talked to her several times a day, worrying about her constantly. She knew they would both feel better if she would come and stay with them at their home but Allyson wouldn't budge. This was where she needed to be.

She watched as Mark Browning drove up her driveway and parked his car. He'd stopped by often, both on duty and off. His kind brown eyes were awash in sympathy every time he looked at her. Sometimes that kindness was hard to take.

He had volunteered to get some of her things at college that she hadn't had time to pack in her rush home. He offered to pack a suitcase for her and pick up the gifts she had bought for her mom's birthday and Christmas presents she would have brought home during winter break.

Mark climbed out of his car carrying her suitcase and a shopping bag and headed to her front door. The reporters yelled questions at him that she couldn't discern. The whole property had been marked off with yellow "no trespassing" tape making it look like a crime had been committed here at the house. Most of the reporters respected the boundaries given to them but a few were arrested for trespassing and whatever other reason the police could find to get them to leave. Just two days before, one climbed the back fence and looked in the window, scaring the crap out of Allyson. She ran out the back door yelling and cursing at them. She imagined her screaming face was by now, plastered on the cover of some tabloid.

Mark knocked softly on the front door and Allyson wiped her wet hands on a kitchen towel and let him inside. He handed her the bag that held her gifts and set the suitcase inside as he closed the door.

"Thanks so much for doing that, Mark. You should be at home sleeping on your time off, not running around doing errands for me," she told him shyly as she watched him take off his dark coat and hang it up. His sandy-brown hair was cut short and standing up a bit over his left ear. She had the strangest urge to reach out and smooth his hair down.

"It was no problem Allyson. I was happy to do it. I wish there was more that I could do for all of you," he said. "For you."

At any other time she might have taken the look he was giving her as attraction but she pushed that thought aside. Don't be ridiculous! she told herself. He was only being nice to her because of the crazy circumstances in her life.

She set the bag of gifts on the dining table. She was a bit unnerved to notice that her heart had started pounding harder at his nearness. Being alone and trying to cope with all this was getting to her. Now she was having romantic notions about a guy who was simply being kind to her!

"Would you like to sit down, Mark? I have some coffee brewing," she told him and gestured to a chair.

Her voice came out sounding tremulous and breathless. She took a deep breath as she poured coffee then handed him a cup and placed one on the table for herself. She hardly ever drank the stuff but lately she'd been drinking whole lot of it. Better to have caffeine than the alcohol her mom kept in a cabinet in the den she supposed.

Despite the sadness in her face and unkempt appearance, she was a lovely girl. Her hair was dark blonde hair and was piled on top of her head at a haphazard angle and her blue-green eyes were lovely, the long dark lashes not quite able to hide the turmoil behind them. She wore jeans and an old sweatshirt that had a painting by the artist Jackson Pollack that she had gotten on a trip to Chicago. The abstracts of greens, yellows and reds were in sharp contrast to her pale face.

"Did you catch those rabbits yourself or did they just latch onto your feet?" Mark asked her with a chuckle in his voice.

"What?" she said, then glanced at the bunny slippers she had on her feet. "Oh! My Mom gave these to me two Christmases ago. I was always complaining about how cold it was in the old house I live in at college. I guess I forget to take them back to school with me."

"What's your degree in?"

"Hopefully I passed my classes this semester and get to graduate in January with a Bachelor in Nursing. I really want to work in the Oncology Department one day and hopefully work with the children who have cancer."

"Did I mention that my Mom died of ovarian cancer when I was fifteen?" he asked her.

She looked at him, surprised by the revelation. The teasing that has been in his warm eyes had had been replaced by sadness and regret. She knew that feeling well.

"I'm so sorry, Mark. I didn't know. It's such a difficult thing to go through. To slowly watch a parent, or any family member for that matter, suffer and die." She reached out to touch his hand and gave it a gentle squeeze. "Did it ever get easier?"

"You still cry about them not being there for you. Maybe that sounds selfish in a way, but I know that my Mom would have wanted to still be here for me if she could. You can find a sense of peace though, believing that they are watching over you," he said, squeezing her hand in return. "My Dad remarried not too long ago. I'm happy for him. It's such a terrible thing to go through. Whenever I see him now, I am overwhelmed with gratitude that he was able to keep going and find love again. It was such a long, difficult road for him. I'm thankful he found the strength to continue on. The people you lose take a part of you with them when they pass away, and I still miss her very much."

Allyson glanced at Mark, he seemed absorbed in his own thoughts. Past memories, perhaps. She knew so little about him. The loss of a parent seemed to have brought them closer, at least for the moment.

Mark had only been part of the Greenway Police department for four years. He did not really know her father Andy while he was alive but had heard of him. By all accounts Andy Anderson had been a wonderful person and father. He glanced at Allyson's lovely face and tried not to feel despair for her. Would she have to go through another tragedy? He started to feel a deep ache in his chest that this sweet girl would be hurt even more.

He decided the best tact was to subtly change the subject.

"It would be a very tough job, taking care of kids who have cancer. I'm not sure I could do it," he said to her after a long pause.

She turned to look at him. "I never thought I could have that kind of career. I wanted to be a graphic designer when I was in high school. When my Dad was first diagnosed, my Mom and I did all the research and called all the cancer institute's, talked to all the doctors and nutritionists. I guess we thought that if we just knew those answers we could help him beat it. He went on a nationwide organ donor registry and we kept thinking it would all be just a waiting game until he was chosen. I discovered a strength in me as I helped my Mom take care of him, that I never knew I had. I wanted to get angry at the world. My Dad tried to stay upbeat through all of this so it was hard to give into that anger. He never complained. He never got mad either, which sometimes made my Mom and I mad," she chuckled. "I know he fought the disease with all the strength he had but I always felt that he accepted it in his own way as well. I don't think my mom and I ever truly have."

Mark covered her hand with his. He didn't know if he would ever find real peace either from losing his Mom.

"I know now that I got that strength from my parents. I know that I can be the best nurse that I can be because of that strength. I have to use that strength to continue believing that my mom is coming home."

***

Eddie finally relented and brought Jane to see Allyson again, although "let" was an understatement. She needed to see for herself that her niece was OK and told him so at every opportunity. Eddie drove her to Anna's house that night, covering her from the cameras as they headed to the front door. He was still irked by all the media melee. It was a constant battle for his police department to keep these vultures away from his family.

He tried not to get too emotional as he watched his wife and beloved niece hold each other for a long moment and then pull apart to wipe away their tears. Jane's face was still heavily bruised but it was starting to look better each day that passed.

They sat on the couch together wrapped in Maria's colorful afghan staring at the blinking lights on the Christmas tree. Allyson was between the two of them, her head on Eddie's shoulder, and Jane held her niece's hand in her own. She had brought dinner and as they'd eaten, Allyson mentioned that Mark had come over earlier that day. Eddie was sure he saw his niece blush as she spoke. He found that curious. Mark and Allyson? Curious indeed.

"It's hard to believe that it's almost Christmas," Allyson said quietly as they sat watching the lights flicker off and on.

Christmas had usually been a happy event for their family. There were festive meals and Grandma and Grandpa Monroe visiting and playing games. Grandpa Monroe singing Christmas carols in his surprisingly deep, baritone voice. And there had been Anna and Andy present at all these happy times. Anna laughing or kidding her brother. Talking to Jane about a favorite recipe or gift. Sharing a new Christmas story with Allyson, just as she had done every single year, making up tales of mice or reindeer or snowmen and jolly Santa's. Anna hugging her parents and kissing Andy under the mistletoe. Like they ever needed a reason, Allyson thought, smiling at the memory. Her parents were always touching each other. Sometimes it was just with a glance across the room. What would it be like to have that kind of love she wondered. She didn't know if it would ever happen for her, but it wasn't something she was interested in thinking about just then. Even if a person did find that kind of love, it was always possible to still lose it.

Her Mom had lost the love of her life. Her father's last coherent thoughts were of his sadness that his wife and daughter would suffer so much from his dying.

"I hope one day the two of you can move on again. Find peace in some way," he'd told her as she sat by his bedside reading to him.

"Dad, I'm not going to talk about that," she had said to him, frowning down at the book.

"When would you like to discuss this, Allyson? Next year?" he asked with a teasing smile on his thin face. She looked down at her hands, trying not to let him see the tears in her eyes.

"Look at me, baby," he'd said gently. *"I know it will hurt forever but don't let that pain grow like a cancerous tumor inside you. Celebrate my life as if it was a great gift given to you for a time then find a way to let me go. Remember how much I do want you to find that happiness again."*

Now, she couldn't imagine as she stared at the family Christmas tree with its happy past contrasting with a traumatic present, truly finding that kind of joy in her future. Especially now. What would her

Dad have thought about all that had happened? Why was it that she felt he would have accepted her mother's disappearance as strange as it was? She could still hear his voice clearly telling her to be happy again. For a second her unwavering certainty that her Mother would return started to unravel from the reality of it all. The impossibility of it all hit her like a ton of bricks. For the briefest moment she almost gave into the full-blown fear that crawled over her chest and made it hurt to breathe. It was all too incredulous.

Her mother would never think like that, Allyson chided herself. Even when her Dad was clearly losing his battle with cancer, Anna had still been searching for a cure. She never gave up hope.

Allyson would somehow hang onto that same hope. If it was possible for her mother to disappear in some crazy way, then it was also possible she could return, wasn't it?

"I believe it will be the year for a Christmas miracle," she said out loud. "Can you feel it?"

Eddie shared a smile with Jane.

"We could certainly use a Christmas miracle," he said and hugged his niece tightly. As much as he was determined to find his sister, each day she remained missing was clearly taking a toll on them all. Every day, he went to work determined to find *something* that would explain her mysterious disappearance. After a week without one tiny piece of additional evidence, Eddie's feelings of confidence had begun to waver. The only thing left to do was pray. Pray for a miracle.

CHAPTER TEN
DECEMBER 21, 2012
12:12 A.M

The first thing Anna Anderson thought when she found herself walking down the middle of a highway alone in the dark was how cold she was. Her black winter coat was too lightweight to be outside for long in this kind of weather. What had she been thinking when she'd put this on to walk? She stopped for a moment, looking around, trying to get her bearings. Where the hell was she? And then in the distance, she recognized the First Presbyterian Church on the right side. Further up the hill, was a stone monument sign that read "Welcome to Greenway, Indiana". She was in her hometown, just outside of town. But, why? The church marquee showed a time of 12:12 am. It was after midnight. What was she doing walking alone? As she stood in the wet snow trying to clear her head, the marquee flashed again, showing the date: December 21st, 2012.

December 21st? Anna struggled to clear her head but all she could draw was a mental blank. She could not remember why she was there or where she'd been last. She put her hands in her coat pockets, hoping for some kind of clue, but found nothing. Anna felt a deep sense of fear pass through her. She only knew she had to get out of this cold. There had to be someone who could help her.

Anna started to walk faster down the highway, her breath creating a misty fog around her head. The night sky was clear and black, the stars twinkling overhead like diamonds on velvet. There was no sidewalks this far outside of town, and her booted feet skidded left and right on the icy road. She didn't want to hurt herself before she could find help, but she was too frightened to slow her pace. It took everything she had just to stay upright and not run screaming towards the town. She finally came up over the small hill that concealed the sign for the town limits of Greenway and Main Street. She could see the small grocery store on the left next to the drugstore. The lights were dim. There was not a single car or person about.

She crossed the street quickly to reach the sidewalk on the left side. The path had been cleared of snow and ice which helped her move faster.

Eddie. She had to find her brother. She desperately tried to remember where the police station was. She had seen it thousands of times, it had been in the same building since before she was born. Why couldn't she remember? Buildings and names were recognizable but her recollection of each of them was disjointed as if the past was fighting with the present.

Trying hard not to give into her escalating panic, she passed Paul's Hardware store and the small cafe owned by Gladys Owens, the retired school teacher. There was Debbie's beauty parlor across the street where she got her hair cut, she remembered. She could see the gas station further down the street where she went with her dad in the family station wagon every Saturday when she was growing up.

The town was decorated for Christmas, Victorian lamp posts standing tall on every corner, each with a wreath in the center. There were jolly snowmen and red nosed Santa's everywhere, and each store window had 'sale' and 'discount' signs. Why did it all seem so foreign to her? She skidded to a stop and grabbed onto a lamp post to keep from falling. Maybe it wasn't the town that was different after all, she thought. Maybe it was her.

***

Mark Browning drove his police car slowly down Washington Avenue. He had gone home to sleep for a few hours before his next shift. Since Anna Anderson had gone missing nine days before, everyone at the police department worked as much as they physically could. Basically, he only slept when he could no longer keep his eyes open. He was glad for the help from the Sheriff's office and the State Police. If not for them, Eddie and Mark would have been utterly overwhelmed by the media attention from Anna's disappearance as well as the constant phone calls and questions by what seemed like every government agency in the state. He was seriously afraid that Eddie was going to haul off and shoot someone in the foot soon. If it had to happen, he thought, please let it be one of those asshole tabloid reporters that made their lives hell.

He ran his fingers through his short sandy brown hair, and rubbed the back of his neck. He was just 28 years old but was starting to feel like an old man. Eddie's patience had been sorely tried with his sister's disappearance and the media attention, but he'd hung in there for the most part and Mark was proud of him. And he was proud to work for a man who was a role model to him.

Turning his car onto Main Street, his head-lights picked up someone standing in the light from a lamppost. They were hanging onto it as if they could no longer stand. A drunk? As he drove closer he could tell it was a woman. He came to a stop and his lights picked out her face.

He drew in a sharp gasp. My God! It was none other than Anna Monroe Anderson staring back at him, her eyes wide with shock.

He slammed on his brakes and threw his car door open and ran to her. His booted feet skidded on the icy street as he reached the spot where Anna stood clutching the lamppost.

"Mrs. Anderson! Are you alright?"

Anna just stood there staring at him. For a second he thought she didn't recognize him.

"Anna? Are you okay?" he tried again, slower so she could read his lips. "Do you need help?" He looked her over carefully. She did not seem to be injured but it was hard to tell in the dim light. She was wearing the same clothes as she'd been described wearing the day of her disappearance. He touched her arm gently. "Let me help you," he said as he guided her from the sidewalk to his car. He could feel the tension in her arm as he held it and a sense of hesitation as he led her to the passenger side of his car.

Mark ran back to the driver's side and got in. He turned on the inside car light and looked at her more closely. She was shivering violently and her face was pale from the cold air. He turned the heater on full blast.

He touched her arm and said carefully, "Are you hurt?" After a long moment, she shook her head "no".

Mark got on the car radio and called in to the office dispatch. "Get Eddie to the office immediately. Right now!" he ordered. He glanced again at his passenger as he started to drive to the police station. She was making small gasps as she continued to shiver. She was definitely in shock. He was a bit in shock himself. How the hell had she survived that violent car crash? How did she end up walking through town in the middle of the night nine days later? And then he thought of Allyson and his heart leapt with joy. Her mother had returned!

CHAPTER ELEVEN

As his Jeep sped towards town, Eddie clutched the wheel as hard as could. The highway was a sheet of ice and it took all his concentration to keep his vehicle from skidding off of it. He was doing close to 90 m.p.h., his police light flashing blue on the dashboard. His wife Jane sat in the passenger seat. He glanced at her and felt an ache of sympathy. He hated frightening her. Jane's face was still bruised and her nose bandaged, but she looked much better than she had just days ago.

He'd gotten the phone call from dispatch just minutes ago. They did not know why Mark Browning ordered him to the office, only that he sounded upset. Eddie had bolted out of bed and thrown on his clothes. Jane would not let him leave her there. They knew the call had to be about Anna. He would wait to call Allyson until he knew for sure. How did he prepare himself and his family for what might lie ahead?

Eddie slowed down as he came towards town, taking the corners far faster than he should have. Finally, the police station came into view and he skidded his car to a stop in front of the brick building. He hurriedly unbuckled his seat belt and got out, then helped Jane from the passenger side. Together, they hurried through the front door.

There was no one about this time of night. He could see a light in an office where the dispatcher worked, and they walked fast towards the back where his own office was located. Through the cubicle's glass windows, he could see Mark Browning handing a paper cup to someone, but could not make out who it was. Mark turned to look at him as he entered the office, and then stepped away and they finally saw the person sitting there.

"Anna! Oh, thank God!" Eddie said as he rushed to his sisters side. He could hear Jane sobbing behind him as he got down on his knees in front of her. He gathered Anna into his arms as she looked up at him, her face full of confusion. As he held her tightly, he finally gave way to the tears that had threatened to spill over the last nine days. Anna stood up shakily and then the three of them held onto each other and cried.

He finally stepped away and wiped his wet face, holding onto her hands, looking her up and down carefully. He saw no signs of obvious injury, her clothes seemed to hang on her as if she'd lost weight. Her hair was disheveled and slightly damp and her face devoid of color except for the small patches of red high on her cheeks. She was shivering slightly, and making small sounds he could not discern.

"Are you alright?" he asked her slowly as he took her face into his hands and stared into her blue eyes. He wanted to scream for joy! She had come back! It couldn't quite get over the impossibility of it all. He tried to calm his racing heart.

"The paramedics are on their way," Mark said. "I called them right before you got here."

Anna seemed to be struggling to answer her brother.

"I don't understand what happened. Why am I here? What was I doing walking outside of town?" she asked slowly as though trying to find her voice. It came out on a shaky whisper.

Eddie motioned for her to sit down. Anna finally got a good look at her sister-in-law's face.

"Jane! What happened to you? Oh my gosh! Were you beaten?" she asked.

Eddie and Jane glanced at each other and something undetectable passing between them. Jane sat down beside her and took Anna's hand. She felt the tears on her own face. Jane could hardly believe what had happened! Wherever Anna had been, or had gone through didn't matter at this moment. She said a private prayer of thanks. Thank goodness they finally had wonderful news to tell Allyson!

"I was in a car accident almost nine days ago," Jane said.

"Are you alright? Was anyone else hurt?" Anna asked her face upturned with a frown.

Eddie stayed quiet through this exchange, his eyes never leaving his sister. There was something different about her. He heard it in her speech. He felt it through her behavior and body language. There was something else he was missing.

Eddie stood up and talked quietly to Mark, who assured him the paramedics would be there soon. Anna needed to be checked over by them immediately and taken to a hospital if necessary.

Anna sat holding Jane's hand as the two men talked. Jane hugged her close and said, "It's going to be OK, Anna".

Eddie walked back to Anna and said softly and carefully, "We are going to get you checked out. Just to make sure you are unhurt."

As Anna looked into his eyes, a trickle of fear went up her spine. She had a vision of the two of them from her past. *She had been just sixteen years old and he was holding her hand. She was lying in a hospital bed. Her face was wet with tears. Eddie was writing something in a note book.*

That's when it hit her.

With a loud gasp, Anna bolted up right out of the chair, and backed away from all of them.

"Anna! Are you alright? What is it? Anna!" they all said at once, moving toward her.

She kept moving away from them, knocking over paperwork and boxes as she fled. She tripped over a file and went sprawling backwards, then fell against the office wall. She felt like her lungs were on fire as she tried to breathe.

Eddie, Jane and Mark rushed to help her, but she put her hands out, warding them off.

"Stop! Stop!" she said. As she looked at their frightened faces she remembered how each one of them had talked to her. How carefully and slowly their speech had been, as if it would help her to understand. It was because she had lost her hearing when she was sixteen years old. She remembered that now. Anna started to sob.

"Don't you see?" she said. "I still don't know what has happened to me, but I remembered what happened to me a very long time ago. I almost died, right Eddie?" she said. "But, I didn't die. I lost my hearing."

Eddie, Jane and Mark continued to stare at her. Eddie took a step closer.

"I think I might be crazy," she continued. Eddie got down on his knees and tried to hold her but she shook her head.

"Anna, you're not crazy. Just something very crazy happened to you," he said.

He still didn't get it, Anna thought. How would she tell them? How could she explain it when she herself had just realized the truth?

"Eddie, go stand out in the hallway where I can't see you," she said.

Her brother looked at her in astonishment. He shook his head, and then did what she'd asked of him anyway.

Anna waited until she could no longer see him. She looked at Jane and Mark who stood there bewildered. Her knees felt like gel as she tried to stand. She took a deep breath and closed her eyes.

"Eddie. Remember what you wrote to me in that notebook so long ago. When I asked you how I could stop being scared of that silence?"

Eddie was taken aback by her question but remembered that conversation well. Why was she asking him this when she couldn't see him? "I said you embrace it," he said from the hall.

"You said I embrace it." she repeated.

Eddie took a step towards his office. He shook his head, not understanding, but continued. "You didn't embrace it for a very long time, Anna. You were just so angry. It was Andy who helped you to do that," he continued sadly.

"It was Andy who helped me to do that," she repeated.

Eddie walked slowly into his office. He had gone through so many emotions these last nine days. Such fear and apprehension, anger and self-doubt as a police officer, husband and brother. As he looked at his sister, suddenly he knew why he had felt that something was off. Something he had not grasped when he talked to Anna. Her speech and body language had been different. Now he knew why.

Anna was standing there with tears running down her face.

"I'm not deaf any more, Eddie," she said.

***

"Does someone need help?" one paramedic asked the group as two of them strolled into the room. The firemen looked around the room at the police chief and his lieutenant and one of them noticed the blonde women standing in the corner.

"Hey! Isn't that Anna Anderson?" he asked, moving closer. "Are you alright, Ma'am?"

"Guys, just give them a moment," Mark Browning said and he ushered the paramedics into the other room, closing the office door.

"I need to sit down," Anna said. She dropped shakily into an office chair, then closed her eyes and took deep a breath.

Not deaf! What the hell? Eddie kept trying to make some sense of it all but his mind was dull from lack of sleep and the toll the last nine days had taken on him. Hell, maybe they were all crazy. She could hear! What an insane, yet truly wonderful thing! Again, how was that possible?

"Anna, what's the last thing you remember?" he asked her finally. Her eyes were still closed but he could tell that she heard him. She heard him! He felt waves of different emotions. Eddie wanted to dance a jig and whoop for joy, yet he could feel in the depths of his soul that there was still something not right. God, he was so damned tired.

Anna opened her eyes and looked at her brother. It had been such a long time since she had heard that gruff, masculine voice. She could hear! Her amazement and extreme gratitude was tempered by puzzlement and even fear. She tried to think back to the past few days but still could not remember. Did she have amnesia? She had no idea when deafness had left and her hearing had returned. How could it be?

Outside the office window snow was coming down in heavy white sheets. She remembered how cold it had been outside. Freezing. Suddenly, she remembered another cold, rainy day.

"I remember Andy's funeral," she said softly. "It was raining. Jane held an umbrella over me as I stood beside his coffin. I hadn't wanted to leave him there alone in the cold."

"That was over three years ago, Anna," Eddie told her gently.

"Tell me what happened, Eddie. What was I doing walking outside of town in the middle of the night?" She looked at him imploringly.

Eddie sighed deeply. He was going to have to explain this to her. Explain the accident again just like he had done with Allyson more than a week ago. Just like he had explained it to the media and reporters over and over the last nine days. He wasn't sure how much stress she could take. She already looked so fragile.

He gathered up the photos from the accident that were still spread on his desk. He moved his chair next to Anna's, and gave her hand a gentle squeeze.

"You and Jane were in a car accident on your birthday," he said as he passed her the accident photos. "When the police and firemen got to the scene of the accident, they helped Jane out of the car and took her to the hospital in an ambulance."

"Was I hurt?" Anna asked, confused. The pictures showed what looked like a violent accident. She was surprised and thankful that Jane had not been more seriously hurt. The passenger side was completely caved in. She shook her head. She did not recall any accident.

Eddie felt Jane's hand on his arm, comforting him.

"We couldn't find you, Anna. It was like you were never in that car at all. But, there was no doubt of that. You were sitting in that car just seconds before the accident occurred."

"I don't understand," she said in bewilderment. "What are you saying? How could I both be there and not there?"

Eddie sighed. "See, I was hoping you could explain that to us, Anna. I was hoping you could tell us how you disappeared at the impact of a car accident. I was hoping you could tell us how you are now sitting here in my office, nine days later. Not just sitting here, but...changed."

CHAPTER TWELVE

Anna did not have an answer. For the life of her, she couldn't think of anything coherent to say.

"Where's Allyson?" Anna said finally. Her daughter must have known that she had been missing. Not just missing. "Oh my god! She must be so frightened!"

"She's at your house now. I'll take you to her in a moment," Eddie said. He wasn't going to get any answers right now. They were all too tired.

He left the room to talk briefly to Mark and the paramedics. He would let them check her but not take her to the hospital that night unless they felt she needed further medical attention. He had to make sure her reappearance stayed confidential for now. When the media got hold of her return it was going to be bedlam. Especially when they learned, as they would, that she had turned up no longer deaf.

"Do me a favor, Mark," Eddie said looking at his lieutenant, after the paramedics went into the office to examine Anna. "Punch me real hard in the face."

"Any other time, boss, I'd be happy to," Mark said. "I think one of us needs a clear head. You can punch me though, if it helps."

They watched through the glass as the paramedics checked Anna's blood pressure and statistics. She had definitely lost some weight since they last saw her and there were visible dark circles under her eyes. Her hair was tangled around her shoulders. Sitting together, Anna and Jane made quite the forlorn pair.

Eddie was amazed and thankful they were both sitting there and not more seriously hurt...or gone. He watched the paramedics talking carefully to Anna who only answered "yes" or "no" to their questions. They didn't know she could now hear each word they spoke to her. The examination complete, they left the room.

"She seems alright," one of them said to Eddie. "I think she's still in a bit of shock but nothing dire. She should get a thorough check up at the hospital or clinic tomorrow, though."

"I'll take care of that" Eddie told them. "Listen, I don't want anyone finding out about this right now. We're going to get a few hours sleep then deal with this later this morning," And he led them towards the door.

Mark left to do some paperwork in the other room. He would have to make a report of tonight's happenings. He would also have to call the Sheriff, State Police and FBI to let them know about Anna Anderson's reappearance. There was no getting around that. She was officially listed as a missing person and a APB was out from her disappearance.

Eddie walked back into his office and stood beside his wife's chair. They watched Anna straighten her clothes and try to smooth her tangled hair. Her face was so white that Eddie wondered if he was making a mistake not taking her to the hospital. She kept smoothing her hair over her left ear over and over, her face growing puzzled, then frantic. Eddie took a step toward her.

"What is it? What's the matter, Anna?" he asked.

"It's gone!" she said, with panic.

"Anna, what is gone?" Eddie and Jane looked at her in concern. What now?

"My implant," she said. And then she started to laugh hysterically. They rushed towards her to hug her close. She was shaking so badly, her teeth rattled.

She'd had a hearing device called a cochlear implant placed just above her left ear when she was 18 years old. The small bump under the skin had been present ever since, something she could feel whenever she washed or brushed her hair or put on her reading glasses. The technology had still been so new then, in the early 1980's. Unfortunately, the surgery had not been successful as the implanted wire had gone to the wrong place. Eddie and his parents had been devastated for her, but Anna shrugged it off angrily. The doctors had wanted her to try again throughout the years as the technology became more advanced and Anna always intended to, but, life had a way of getting busy. She went off to college, met Andy, got married and started her career as a reference librarian. When baby Allyson came along, things revolved around their child. "Someday" had become "never". And now this implanted device was gone. It was too much.

"I want to go home now," Anna said as she put her coat on. "I need to see my daughter."

***

As Eddie drove his Jeep through the back roads of Greenway towards his sister's house, his pace was much slower than it had been two hours before on the way to town. He kept one eye on the road and another on Anna in the backseat via his rearview mirror. It would not surprise him at all if he looked back in a moment and she was no longer there. Nothing at all would surprise him ever again. As he drove, he told Anna about all the frenzied media attention her disappearance had caused and tried to prepare her for that onslaught to come. One thing at a time, he told himself. Eddie thought of his niece and the huge shock she was in for. He wished he could mentally prepare her for all of this but there was just no way anyone could.

Anna sat in the back seat listening to the gentle swooshing noise the heater gave off, the crunch the tires made on the snow; the thunk-thunk that the windshield wipers made on the glass windshield. She thought she could hear her own heart thudding in erratic beats. It was such an incredible miracle that was so difficult to process. She put her head in her hands and breathed slowly, trying not to break into sobs. Why couldn't she remember what had happened?

Finally, the street she lived on came into view. The snow was coming down heavily and the back roads had not yet been plowed. Eddie carefully pulled into Anna's driveway, the car's tires digging deeply into the new snow. The lines of yellow tape gave him a strange urge to run into the house and grab Allyson, then haul her into the car and with all of them together, take off and head out of town. Eddie sighed and turned off the engine.

"How do I do this?" Anna asked them quietly from the backseat.

"Just like ripping off a band-aid quickly," Jane said, reaching out to hold Anna's small hand with her own. Anna grasped it tightly. "But it's not going to be painful, just...shocking. She'll be so happy to see you!"

"It's not like any of us have been shocked lately," Eddie said sardonically as he undid his seatbelt.

All three of them got out of the vehicle and walked to the front of the house. Eddie used his key to unlock the door. He looked back at Anna, and let her go in first.

As Anna looked around the entryway of her beloved home she felt a flood of emotion at the memories of her family life all around her. She felt Andy everywhere. His contagious smile and his warm hugs. The way he had smelled when he held her and how he made her and Allyson laugh with his goofiness and terrible jokes. How she missed him!

There was Andy rushing down the stairs on his way to work. He always wore a suit and tie to his job of teaching history at the local high school. How handsome he was with his dark hair and green eyes and his ever-present smile. Andy coming in the front door after a game of basketball with his church league, sweaty and red faced, bemoaning the lousy play of his teammates. Andy giving a four-year-old Allyson a piggy back ride on his shoulders, skipping along like a pony. Andy helping an older Allyson with her homework at the dining table. Andy looking up at her admiringly as she came down the stairs dressed for a night out with him. Andy standing there holding a bouquet of roses and saying, "I love you, princess."

He had loved life so much. Had it really been three years since she had stood at this entryway after coming home from his funeral? It felt like yesterday that she had walked inside her front door and felt the searing pain of loneliness and loss.

She struggled to control her feelings but it was all too much. She felt the hot tears run down her cheeks as she stifled a sob. And then she felt hands laid comforting on her shoulder. Through her tears, she could see the colorful outline of the Christmas tree in the den. There was a nightlight in the corner, the little Santa decoration casting a small red glow. On the old family couch was her daughter, asleep, bundled up in her grandmother Maria's afghan. How beautiful her child was!

She must have gasped out loud because Allyson suddenly opened her eyes and looked right at her. And then she bolted off the couch and threw herself into her mother's arms.

"Mom! Mom! Oh, thank God! "Allyson sobbed as she held Anna tightly. As they rocked each other back and forth, Anna caressed her daughter's hair.

Allyson pulled away from her. "Where have you been? Are you alright? What happened?" She wiped tears from her cheeks. "Am I awake?"

Hearing her daughter's voice for the first time was so overwhelming, she wanted to sink to her knees in joy. Anna almost laughed out loud! Her voice *was* exactly the way she always imagined it. There had been so many times of frustrating communications when Allyson was growing up. When she was a young child and frustrated by not knowing how to sign a certain word to her mother or the countless times she had had to interpret a phone caller for Anna or explained uncaptioned television shows. The times Allyson signed for her when they went shopping or out to eat and all those times as a turbulent teenager that she would rather tell her mother "just forget it" than try and communicate to her the problem she was having. Anna knew it had all been just the age she had been going through and nothing to do with their relationship. That's what she had told herself at the time, anyway.

There were times of laughter and happiness as well, no matter how challenging their communications were. The times they secretly signed to each other in a dark movie theatre and stifled their laughter as they made fun of a character or the cheesy dialogue that had come up on the captioned screen. She remembered when she would tell Allyson stories completely in sign, lying in a blanket tent in Allyson's bedroom with nothing but a flashlight to shadow their hands. Anna knew in her heart that her daughter had always been proud of her, proud of her strength and capabilities.

And now, for some yet unknown reason, they were given a second chance to mend the bond that had been cracked when Andy passed away. Whatever had happened to Anna, there was truly a miracle involved somehow and she was so grateful for this moment, for this wonderful gift.

CHAPTER THIRTEEN

"Let's sit down," Eddie said. He hugged the two of them together tightly for a brief moment. Watching the two had lifted his heart from the heaviness it endured the last nine days. What a relief it was! Anna had returned!

Anna put her arm around her daughter's shoulder and guided her onto the seat of the worn couch. More memories hit her as she regarded the tree. So many Christmases in this house. They had lived here since Allyson was three. Nineteen years. Anna took a deep breath and looked again at her daughter.

"I'm alright sweetheart. Just really, really tired. I know you are going to want answers about where I have been and what happened. Right now, I don't know those answers," Anna said. Eddie and Jane took off their coats and sat on the loveseat on the other side of the room. They looked beyond exhausted.

"I found myself walking outside of town a bit after midnight. Just walking in the middle of the street in the snow. That's the first thing I remember. I don't know how I got there or why. I remember feeling so confused and disoriented. It was so cold and no one was about. I walked up the hill into town and starting walking on the sidewalk. That's when Mark Browning, the police lieutenant, found me as he was driving past. He took me to the police station and called your uncle," she continued. Allyson sat there wide eyed and shaking her head in puzzlement, wanting to ask her own questions

"I don't know how I got there Allyson. Maybe it will come to me. Right now I just need to rest and sleep and hold you," Anna said and stroked her daughter's soft hair.

"It's going to be OK, Mom," Allyson said tearfully. "I don't care about anything else. You are here safe and I'm so thankful!"

Anna pulled her daughter close. What a shock it all must have been for her!

After awhile, she stood up and walked to the tree, looking at the ornaments they'd accumulated over the years. A lovely, artificial pine they had bought over ten years ago, it stood tall but slightly leaning to the right. The angel that had belonged to her own Grandma Monroe was proudly perched on top. The angel was dressed in a flowing white robe adorned with tiny white pearls, her white wings spread wide and graceful. It had a tranquil smile on her face and tiny blue painted eyes that seemed to be looking straight at her. Anna wistfully wished she could somehow find the answers she needed there.

She glanced at a small photo framed in the belly of a snowman ornament. It was a picture of Anna, Andy and a baby Allyson. Written on the snowman's scarf were the words, "Baby's First Christmas, 1990". She could remember every detail of that day they took this picture, yet she stood there twenty-two years later and couldn't remember where she had been just days or even hours before.

That sweet baby had grown up into a beautiful, confident and independent young woman who was looking at Anna with love and gladness shining in her eyes.

Anna knelt in front of Allyson. "Something else happened to me, Allyson. Again, I don't know why or how, only that it did," she said. "I don't even know how to explain it, but it is something I am so glad to have." She squeezed her daughters hands.

"I didn't realize it when they first found me on the street in town or in the police car. I didn't even realize it at the police station after your

Uncle Eddie and Aunt Jane arrived. It wasn't until I began to notice how everyone was talking to me that something was not right. How each word they all spoke was said carefully and slowly so that I could lip-read them," she drew in a deep breath and continued. "I remembered it then Allyson. I remembered being deaf. Only, then did I also realize that I...that I...wasn't any longer. I could hear every word they said. I have heard every sound since I found myself walking outside of town. I have heard my feet crunching in the snow as I skidded along the road. I heard my fast breathing and gasping as I walked up the hill. I heard a dog barking somewhere as I entered town and I heard the ice falling off the buildings onto the sidewalks as I walked onto them. I heard Mark Browning calling me and talking to me when he found me clinging to a lamppost in town. I heard the radio chatter in the police car and I heard the clock ticking on the wall and even the fax machine beeping in the next room when we got to the station. I heard your Uncle Eddie and Aunt Jane as they came in and the wonderful sound of their voices. I heard the paramedics talking to me, unbeknownst to them that I could hear every question they asked me. I heard the sounds Eddie's Jeep made as I rode in it on the way over here. I heard the key unlock in our front door and I heard the sound of our furnace as it came on after we walked in." She took in a deep breath.

"Most of all I heard your sweet wondrous voice for the first time and I wanted to fall to my knees at that moment and thank God for such a gift," she told her as the tears flowed down her cheeks.

Allyson's mouth came open, letting out a gasp of shock. She let go of her mother's hands, "*What?* I am not sure that *I* heard you!" She stood up and pushed away from her. And then she stood looking at her like she was some stranger.

"Stormy, it's going to be ok," Eddie told her as he moved towards his niece. He wished they could have found some easy way to tell her all of this, but how could this crazy thing even be explained? He still hadn't grasped it all himself.

"It's a wonderful thing, Allyson!" Jane said, trying to soothe her.

"It's a miracle!"

Anna felt herself start to tremble. What had she done? She just added to her daughters agitation with another earthquake of emotional declaration.

"I'm so sorry, baby. I tried to tell you as gently as I could. I just didn't know how," she told her.

Allyson felt faint. She stepped away from her mother but tripped on the ottoman and dropped to the floor and sat there with her head on her knees. She crossed her arms across her chest and rocked herself.

Eddie got down beside her and took her in his arms as she started to cry. Jane held Anna, who had started to sob, Was this the breaking point for them, he wondered? But then Allyson stood up and wiped her tears from her face and sniffed loudly.

"I know that you would never joke about such a thing, Mom," she said to Anna brokenly. "It must be true." Then she walked towards her and held out her arms. Allyson was her mother's daughter. She would be strong no matter the circumstances. Even crazy, unexplainable ones.

***

Anna stood in her bathroom looking in the mirror. It was the first time she saw herself since before she found herself walking outside of town. Jane, Eddie and Allyson were asleep now. Allyson was asleep in her mother's bed in the next room and Eddie and Jane were sleeping in Allyson room down the hall.

Earlier, each of them mentally pushed away the questions and uncertainties of her disappearance and how Anna returned from wherever she had been for now. They avoided delving too deep into the puzzlement they still all felt. All that would have to wait. It was a time of celebration. Jane whipped up pancakes and decorated the whole stack with cream cheese frosting and a tiny candle in the middle. They sang "Happy Birthday" to Anna as she listened in wonder to their voices.

A few times they had reverted to sign language to talk to her and each other. After they did they'd glance at each other and awkwardly laugh. Old habits would be hard to break.

Now, as Anna glanced at herself in her mirror, first thing she noticed was that she'd lost weight, she could only guess at how much without a scale. Her face was thinner and her clothes hung on her as if made for someone else. A memory of a tiny Allyson dressing up in her clothes when she was in grade school came to her. Her daughter's sweet little girl face triumph as she stood in front of Anna, wearing one of her old dresses and high heeled shoes and signing, "*look at me!*". Her mother's make-up had also been smeared all over her cherubic face. How could you get upset when your six year old dumps $100 worth of cosmetics out yet stands there jubilantly announcing that "she is as 'boo-tee-ful' as her Mommy"?

Precious memories of her family were starting to trickle back to her. The memories of her time with Andy were freshest in her mind, still so painful that when she thought of them, her chest felt like a straight jacket had been tightened across her heart. His presence was ingrained into the soul of this house. Everywhere she looked, each room and corner, each piece of furniture, brought up an image of him from the past.

She sighed and looked closer at her reflection. The skin on her face, although pale and with deep shadows under her eyes, looked firm, and the lines around her eyes and mouth that had grown visible the last few years were so fine that she had to lean close to the mirror to find them. She saw just a hint of them as she gave her reflection a half-hearted smile.

She took off her clothes slowly and rubbed her neck. Every muscle in her body ached as badly as if she'd just finished an intense workout at the gym. She looked down at herself and let out a quiet gasp then turned hurriedly back to the mirror. Her breasts were high and firm. They were not the breasts of a 50-year-old woman. She had always been in pretty good shape and had aged well but some things like gravity and getting older had been beyond her control. She looked more closely at her body and discovered the fine white stretch marks that had appeared on her hips after her pregnancy with Allyson, were also gone.

"What now?" she asked her image and laughed out loud, covering her mouth so as not to wake her daughter. This was yet another thing she couldn't explain. But she certainly wasn't going to question suddenly firm breasts.

She turned on the water in the shower stall and walked inside. She stood still for a moment, listening to the sounds the water made washing over her tired body. It would likely take a long time before being able to hear came close to feeling like a normal part of her life again. As she washed her hair she again felt the uneasiness of not feeling the implant under her skin above her ear. These things just couldn't disappear, but again neither should people. Perhaps for some reason, it was just not detectable for the moment. Anna shook herself mentally at this train of thought. It just was not possible. None of it was.

She got out of the shower and dried off. Wrapping a towel around herself she stood at the sink and brushed her teeth. As she opened her mouth so the brush could reach her molars, she noticed something odd. All of her silver fillings were missing. Her teeth looked perfect.

As she stood there grasping the toothbrush the fear she first felt when she'd stood alone on the highway outside of town washed over her again in disconcerting waves. Too many things were different. She *was* different. Who was this woman staring back at her with dread in her eyes?

CHAPTER FOURTEEN

In the morning Jane made scrambled eggs, toast and coffee. Everyone ate so quietly that Anna thought for a minute she might have only imagined her hearing was back, but then a floorboard would creak, a knife would clink against glass, the furnace would make a loud humming noise and she'd feel herself shaking in surprised anxiety yet again. She wondered if this state of constant shock she felt would ever leave. It was all still a lot to adjust to.

Eddie, Jane and Allyson watched her constantly. Now that everyone had gotten some sleep, Anna knew the time had come to try and make some sense of it all.

"I'm going to need to take you to the hospital as soon as we are done here," Eddie said, putting down his coffee cup. "You'll need to have a full physical. After that, you'll have to come to the police station and make another statement. This time there will be other officers there along with the Sheriff and state police and the FBI."

Anna sat quietly, looking out the dining room window. The sky was a clear blue.

"Do you still not remember anything?" Eddie asked her. He had a gut feeling that a whole lot of things were...just off. As a police officer, he'd learned to pay attention to that feeling.

"I'm starting to remember small things," she said. "Memories of being here after Andy's funeral and the months that followed. I can't recall much after that." She shook her head. "I don't remember the holidays after he passed away or birthdays...or work. I don't even remember spending time with my own daughter, with all of you. I felt like I disappeared the day of Andy's funeral, not on my 50th birthday." The pain was still so fresh and new. It should have grown into a dull misery after three years, shouldn't it?

Anna looked around the table at her family, each watching her with concern. She wanted so much to find joy and celebration in her return but she felt like she hadn't laughed in years. Some way she needed to find that strength again and try and move on. To try and embrace this time with the people she loved.

She turned to Allyson. "I think there are some things all of you should know before everything gets crazier here with the reporters and doctors. Allyson, I know that not much should surprise you anymore, but I noticed other changes about myself on top of no longer being deaf. Remember the ear implant I had when I was still a teenager?" she asked her.

"The one that you've had since you were in high school or something?" Allyson asked.

"Yes," she said, "It's gone."

"Gone? What do you mean?" Allyson asked, her eyes widening in surprise.

She reached out and ran her hand over the spot behind her mother's left ear where she'd always felt when she'd brushed her mother's hair as a little girl. Her dad Andy had called it the "Bionic Mother Meter" capable of transmitting electronic pulses every time a fib came out of their child's mouth. Allyson knew the bionic meter didn't work as she had secretly tested it often. The implant had been a familiar part of her mother's landscape and its disappearance was a shock.

"There's more," Anna said and glanced at Eddie and Jane. "I noticed last night when I was brushing my teeth that all my silver fillings were gone. My teeth look perfect."

For now, she'd keep the disappearing stretch marks and perky breasts to herself.

Allyson rose abruptly from her chair and strode into the den. From there, she began to laugh, a sound that bordered on hysteria.

"Is that all, Mom?" she called. "I mean, is that *it*? Any other bombs you want to drop? I'd prefer them all at once, thank you very much!"

Anna followed her into the room, where she found her daughter curled up on the couch, clutching the afghan to her chest.

"Maybe you need to see a doctor too, sweetheart. This is a shock to all of us," Eddie said from behind her.

"I don't need a doctor, Uncle Eddie!" Allyson shouted. "I don't need a shrink to tell us that we are all f..f... freaking crazy!" Why did she still feel like a kid in her mother's presence, unable to lash out in obnoxious verbal vulgarity?

Eddie's cell phone rang and he left the room to answer it. Anna sat beside Allyson and held her, stroking her hair. The two of them sat there looking at the unlit Christmas tree, struggling to control their emotions.

Eddie came back into the den, holding his phone. "That was Mark on the phone," he said to Anna. "We have to go to the hospital now. We need to get this over with before the reporters get hold of your return.

Jane came out of the kitchen, wiping her hands on a dish towel. "I'm going too," she told Eddie.

Eddie rummaged in the hallway closet and pulled out a dark scarf, which he thrust at Anna.

"Put this on your head. Oh, and wear sunglasses," he told her.

Anna grabbed the scarf from him, shaking her head at his bossiness. But she suspected it might be a long time before the sound of his voice began to irritate her, she thought with a small smile on her face.

"I feel like a blonde Jackie O," Anna grumbled as they went out the front door.

Thankfully the yard was clear of reporters. Once they got to the hospital, that was going to change. Someone was bound to break the news that Anna Anderson had shown up after missing for nine days.

Eddie was glad for the Jeep's tinted windows as he drove toward the hospital. Jane sat in the front seat beside him. He could feel her watching him. The sun was shining on the newly laid snow. It was a beautiful morning. He carefully drove past a snow plow working overtime to clear the streets. A layer of ice underneath made driving tenuous. He could hardly believe that the night before, he'd driven a street even more treacherous than this at 90 mph. Way to be a well-rounded, law abiding citizen, chief of police Monroe! He told himself. Jane squeezed his hand and he turned and smiled at her.

"I guess you should all know," said Anna from the back seat, "that, well...I don't need prescription sunglasses anymore." She waited for someone to say something but no one said a word.

She looked out the tinted windows at the winter wonderland. It really was a lovely day. Her newly perfect eyesight took it all in, the snow and Christmas decorations.

"Let me see now," Eddie finally said, "Perfect hearing, perfect teeth and eyesight. We have almost conquered all the senses here. How's your taste?"

"It's kind of bland actually," Anna quipped.

"Don't worry, I think that's just Jane's cooking," Eddie said and smirked.

"Eddie!" Jane blushed as she affectionately smacked his shoulder.

The four of them laughed heartily. It felt so good to let go and feel something else besides confusion and trepidation and that constant engulfing sense of fear.

Eddie turned on the radio and Christmas music piped in from the speakers. He started to sing along in his manly baritone voice.
We three kings of Orient are;
Bearing gifts we traverse afar,
Field and fountain, moor and mountain,
Following yonder star.

Anna smiled misty eyed as Allyson and Jane joined in. They'd sung this carol every Christmas Eve when she was a little girl. She'd play the song, her family and grandparents joining in, standing around the piano.

Now, she joined their singing too, tentatively at first, her voice cracking in the first couple of verses. Her voice still had the slight speech impediment that made her sound like she had a chest cold or that English was her second language, not her first. She grew braver as the song went on, letting herself feel each word. Andy once told her that music came from within her soul, not only from listening to the sound of it, as he held her and they danced their first dance. Anna had stopped allowing music to be a big part of her life as a teenager but she never really forgot all the songs she'd heard. Each song was still ingrained in her memory like a tiny birthmark on her skin. Permanent and everlasting.

Westward leading, still proceeding,
Guide us to thy perfect light.

***

Anna, Allyson and Jane sat in the hospital waiting room while Eddie went to talk to the staff about setting up her physical. He also had called Anna's own physician, dentist and eye doctors, who had agreed to come in at once. Eddie didn't tell them anything about her reappearance or physical changes. Anna noticed that the staff were whispering and staring at her. Jane and Allyson sat opposite, creating a barrier of protection from curious eyes.

When Mark Browning came in the waiting room, his soft brown eyes lit up when he saw Allyson sitting with her mother. Anna watched her daughter get up and hug him, surprised at the look of pleasure on her face. She thought Mark was a handsome, sweet young man. He'd always spoken to her with kindness the few times she'd talked to him.

"How are you doing, Mrs. Anderson?" Mark asked turning to look at her.

"I'm OK," she said. "thanks, Mark. Please call me Anna."

He turned back to Allyson. "I'm so happy for you," he said. "This is incredibly wonderful news!"

"Thanks so much, Mark," she replied shyly. "We are all a little overwhelmed."

Anna and Jane shared a quizzical look. These two definitely liked each other. Anna hid a smile with her hand.

When Eddie came in, he found his lieutenant holding his niece a little too closely for his liking. They were going to have to have a talk about that, he thought.

"The media has gotten hold of the story of Mrs. Anderson's...uh, Anna's reappearance." Mark told Eddie, stepping quickly away from Allyson. "The State police and Sheriff's deputies are on their way here so we'll have some kind of control outside the hospital. It's going to be bedlam out there in a few minutes. No one will be allowed to enter the west wing of this hospital for now unless they are employees or residential staff. We've also blocked off the street where Anna lives."

A young nurse wearing green scrubs entered the room and gestured to the open door and hallway beyond. "Mrs. Anderson, we're ready for you now. Will you come this way please?" she said looking straight at Anna.

"I'm going with her," Allyson said. She was not going to let her mother out of her sight. The two followed the nurse down a long hallway and into a small examining room.

The nurse was very young and pretty with dark red hair and brown eyes. She also looked extremely nervous. Her name tag on her green scrubs showed her name as Jennifer, L.P.N. "Mrs. Anderson, I'm going to take your temperature, weight and blood pressure," she spoke to Anna carefully. The hospital staff had not been told she was no longer deaf.

An overwhelming sense of apprehension had come over Anna as she'd entered the room. Why was she so afraid? The physical was the first step in finding out the truth about her disappearance and what happened to her in those nine days she went missing. Anna was somehow afraid of that truth. Sometimes reality was more difficult to face than the pretension that everything was okay.

CHAPTER FIFTEEN

"Mom, are you alright?"Allyson asked as she reached out to touch her mother's shoulder. "I'm fine," Anna said, shrugging. "Let's get it over with."

Jennifer, the young nurse, took Anna's temperature and blood pressure. When Anna had stepped on the scale it showed she'd had a weight loss of 15 pounds since her last physical just a month earlier, according to her health records. Anna tried not to gasp out loud at that number. Her weight had been almost always steady throughout her life except for a couple years after her pregnancy. Staying in shape after the age of 40 had become more and more difficult. It took a lot longer to work off a pound or two then it had years ago. She reminded herself that she was over 50 now. Just because she missed the damn birthday didn't mean it hadn't happened.

"How are you feeling today, Mrs. Anderson?" the nurse asked as she wrote in her file. "Are you having any pain anywhere?"

"No pain. All things considered, I'm doing fine, thanks."

"Could you please get undressed and put on this gown and sit on the exam table?" the nurse asked as she handed her a paper gown. "The doctor will be here in just a moment," she said and left the room, closing the door after her.

"I'll be right outside the door, Mom," Allyson told her, giving her an encouraging look.

Anna sighed as she took off her clothes and put on the paper gown. How was anyone supposed to keep their dignity wearing such a stupid piece of paper? She felt it tear across her breasts as she sat down on the exam table. Great. Just great.

As she lay back on the exam table trying to clear her head, holding the silly gown together as best as she could, Anna felt herself begin to tremble, her breathing going from a steady quiet rhythm to thudding gasps. The apprehension she had felt coming into the room had started to escalate into a full-blown panic attack.

She sat up and bolted off the exam table. She had to get out of there, now! She ripped off the gown and put her clothes back on, her hands shaking. As she grabbed her purse and opened the door, a young doctor was coming in.

"Mrs. Anderson! Are you alright?" he asked as she ran past him.

"Mom! Mom!" she could hear Allyson yelling after her as she ran down the hallway, trying to find the exit.

Anna rushed through the doors to the waiting room, gasping to find Eddie, Jane, Mark and another doctor standing there looking at her in surprise.

"I'm not doing this, Eddie! I'm not going to do this!" she yelled. Her voice boomed in the small room, hurting even her own ears.

"Anna! Anna! It's OK, sweetheart. It's OK!" Eddie said as he moved towards his sister. She'd seemed to be fine all morning. Now she stood before him, her face white with anxiety.

"I want to go home! I want to go home now!" she said lowering her voice to panicked sobs. She clutched her hands together, rocking herself back and forth.

"We're going to go home now, Mom," Allyson said soothingly as she took Anna in her arms and hugged her tight. And she looked at her uncle, defying him to argue otherwise. They had been wrong to bring her here, it was too soon. Her own heart was thudding in her chest. She'd never seen her mom so afraid. The woman who had been a tower of strength throughout Allyson's life, even through her Dad's cancer, was now terrified.

"Let's get out of here," she said.

***

They left through a back door and managed to elude the press at the front. The trip home was quiet, except for Anna's stifled sobs from the backseat. She sat wedged between Allyson and Jane, both trying to comfort her.

What the hell had he done? Eddie berated himself as he drove. He had been thinking like a police officer, and not as her brother. Talking to her this morning, she'd seemed upbeat and cheerful, even. Whatever she'd felt in the exam room had caused her enough anxiety to run screaming back to the waiting room demanding to leave. Eddie knew without a doubt his sister was not OK.

Mark drove a police car in front of them. A couple of state police officers had been asked to help control the media that Eddie knew were already descending on the street Anna lived. Thank goodness she lived on a cul-de-sac with few neighbors. So far her neighbors were understanding and patient but now Eddie imagined these neighbors were going to lose that patience very quickly after today.

As he turned off the highway onto Anna's street, he saw a sea of reporters, news vans and cameras. It was indeed bedlam. There must have been more than fifty TV station news vans, and he could hear the distinctive noise of helicopters above them. The two state police officers looked overwhelmed. His whole town seemed to have been descended on by a swarm of ego-driven, microphone welding locusts. There was nowhere to turn without being set upon by all them at once.

A mob of them rushed at the cars as they inched slowly toward the street blockade, thrusting their cameras at the windows. Mark turned his siren on, the noise of it momentarily drowning out the voices from the screaming herd of press as they shouted out questions.

As they finally got through the blockade, Eddie sighed in relief. He was going to have to ask for even further help from other city police stations. Hell, all the police in nearby Indianapolis couldn't control this mass of self-absorbed humanity. He was all for freedom of the press, but not when it took over his town or involved his family.

In front of Anna's street. Mark turned and parked his police car sideways on the other side of the blockade as they went past him. Many of her neighbors had come out to see what was going on. Eddie pulled into Anna's driveway, thankful he had remembered to grab the garage door opener on the hallways table before they left. Inside the garage, the four of them sat in stunned silence as the door went down, closing out the noise from outside.

"I'm so sorry, Anna," Eddie said, turning to look in the backseat. "I should have waited. I tried to rush to get this done before the these vultures descended but I only brought attention to your return."

"I...I..I'm going to be fine, Eddie," Anna said. "I don't know what came over me. It's not your fault. I was ready to go too. Ready to get it over with," she offered him a soft. "I'm home now. It's all going to be OK. It's going to be fine."

She repeated these words over and over as Jane and Allyson helped her out of the Jeep and into her house. Eddie watched them take her up the stairs to her room, as she kept whispering "it's going to be fine, it's all OK."

He thought all of them knew differently.

Eddie called Mark on his cell phone to discuss the crowds and let him know he'd be down there in a few minute to make his "no official comment" to the reporters and ask them to be considerate of their privacy and of the neighbors. He also asked Mark to call Sheriff Cole to see if the State Police could offer more help. Certainly, this was an emergency of great proportions. He imagined himself standing before the Board of town Trustees trying to convince them that the funds he'd used for overtime and extra security was intended for a doomsday media apocalypse.

As he entered Anna's house, he could hear the news helicopters flying overhead. That was another thing he'd have to try and deal with. That one might be a lost cause. There was no crime being done as they sought out a story. As he climbed the stairs to the second floor he could hear Allyson and Jane talking soothingly to Anna. God, he felt terrible.

Anna was in her bed, dressed in pajamas and Jane and Allyson were sitting with her.

"I'll make some tea," Jane said. As she got up and walked past Eddie she gave him a brief hug.

Eddie sat down on the bed beside Anna and took her cold hand. She looked somewhat better than she had in the car. At least he wanted to convince himself that she did. She laid there clutching the pillow that had been Andy's. The pillow she had never been able to throw away.

Anna's captioned phone sat on the bedside table, unplugged, beside a family photograph of the Anderson family that was taken at Allyson's High School graduation. Andy had been sick then, slim and pale, his dark suit hanging on him just a bit from the weight he had lost. But, he was standing tall and smiling ear to ear, one armed wrapped around his beloved daughter in her blue graduation cap and gown, the other arm hugging Anna close. It was a lovely picture of the three of them with only a slight sense of something wrong from the trying-too-hard smiles of Anna and Allyson. Andy had died less than 18 months from that special day.

"I'm sorry, sweetheart," Eddie told his sister.

For a moment, Anna thought he was talking about Andy. Then she remembered.

"I know, Eddie," she said, turning to look at her brother, "It's not your fault. I overreacted at the hospital. I know it's something that needs to be done, but right now I just want to be home with my family. Maybe even enjoy Christmas."

Eddie bent down and kissed her forehead, glad that she could think about a thing like a holiday.

"We'll sing Christmas songs and suffer through Jane's cooking, and maybe even get real drunk," Eddie said and gave her a grin.

"I heard that!" Jane called up the stairs. The three of them looked at each other and chuckled.

"I need to go back to work now. Apparently something crazy is going on in our small town." He smiled as he stood up. "I have no idea how any of that went on without the knowledge of Greenway's police chief."

"Finally proof, big brother, that you indeed don't know everything," Anna said, smiling up at him. He shook his head and started to say something, but thought better of it. It did his heart good just to see her smile.

"I love you, Anna."

"I love you too, Eddie," she said a little surprised. They'd said the words to each other often but he'd had said this with such a current of emotion, she worried he would actually break down in tears.

He waved at the two of them as he left the bedroom and headed downstairs.

"Are you ever going to stop making fun of my cooking?" Jane asked him in the kitchen.

"Honey, that's all I got going for me at the moment. Humor," he said holding her close. "Plus a really good police gun. But the town tends to frown upon its law-abiding officials running amok and breaking a few laws, so I'm opting to be funny."

"At least one person in this house thinks you are," Jane smirked.

"Now that's just mean, Mrs. Monroe," he chuckled and kissed her. He put on his coat and went outside to the garage. Time to get back to work. Time to deal with the insanity.

CHAPTER SIXTEEN

Anna sighed with frustration as she looked over the mess she'd made in the small attic. Boxes were opened everywhere, their contents spilling out like paper guts at a recycling factory.

There had to be something in the house that had Andy's voice on it! She grumbled in frustration.

She tried to block the memory of yesterday's hospital visit from her mind. The overwhelming anxiety she'd felt as she lay there on the exam table threatened to engulf her all over again. She was still embarrassed about how she had lost it, scaring her family and making a scene in a public place.

Eddie and Jane decided to sleep over once again, and they and Allyson had not yet woken. They were all so mentally and physically exhausted. She hoped she wouldn't wake them with her search but this was something she needed to do.

She couldn't stop thinking about how wonderful it would be to finally hear Andy's voice after all these years. She tried to hold back the tears as she unearthed the box of albums that held their wedding pictures and other photos of their life together in her home office closet earlier. There were boxes of Andy's high school and college awards and mementos, ribbons and trophies from track meets and clubs. She had found his gray Indiana Mid-western University sweatshirt that smelled slightly of mildew and moth-balls, but she put it on over her pajamas anyways. It warmed the coldness she felt throughout her body ever since her return. She still found herself shivering so violently at times she had to hug herself to keep the spasms at bay.

They used to have an answering machine, before the invention of cell phones. Andy had recorded himself singing lines to "Ring My Bell" on the outgoing message. He'd shown her the lyrics and assured her that he'd sung it with melodious rhythm and 'cool dude' artistry. She remembered talking about it with a ten-year-old Allyson as she sat at the dining table doing her homework.

"Mother, he stinks," she had signed then said. "It sounds like a cat got its tail caught in Dad's weed whacker. I am totally embarrassed when my friends call."

"I saw that, young lady! No one but me appreciates my musical tone," he'd said looking forlornly at Anna. She had noticed the twinkle in his beautiful green eyes and saw that he couldn't quite hide his amusement.

"Dammit!" she muttered in growing anger as she looked around the attic again. There had to be something! Didn't they have an old video camera and tapes? Andy's parents had died years ago and he was an only child. They'd inherited boxes of their possessions. If there was anything with his voice on it, it would be here in this house. She pulled open another small box and looked inside. She closed her eyes at the contents. All the personal items from Andy's hospital room were there. All the cards and letters from his family and friends and high school students. There were prayer books and pictures of angels and small cards with hymns from well meaning church friends. She gently put them aside and dug a little deeper. As she put a get well card out of the way she saw a box containing a small digital picture player. Anna picked it up as if it was fragile then carefully opened the box and took it out. Staring at the blackness of the blank screen, she felt for the on switch at the back. As it came to life, Anna remembered the last time she had played it.

***

It had been their 25th anniversary. The two of them sat at a small table in Andy's hospital room. It was a beautiful summer night. The curtains were open so they could see the stars twinkling over a park directly opposite the hospital and visible from his room. A gentle breeze blew in the scent of the gardenias that grew along the park entrance. Allyson and the hospital staff had decorated the room with flowers and balloons and a small banner over the bed that read "Happy 25th Anniversary!". There were candles on the table and a white lace cloth. Allyson had also gone to the trouble to pick up Anna's favorite meal from a local steak house, and brought a couple of pieces of the family's heirloom china from home to serve the food on. Andy just recently had another round of chemotherapy and he was still on a liquid diet, so there was a soup dish filled with clear broth for him. He sat at the table in his good robe and pajamas, looking thin and pale. The dark bruises under his eyes were testament to his sleepless nights.

He'd given her a locket as a gift. Inside was a picture of them on their wedding day. They looked so happy, radiant and overjoyed. They'd felt that day that they had a whole lifetime of happiness ahead of them. Days filled with work and play, family and vacations and watching their child grow up. One day retiring and buying a home near the beach, sitting and rocking on the porch, holding their grandchildren. They had certainly done many of these things together but not nearly enough. Life seemed to have gone by so quickly, zooming by like a speeding train with only a few stops. Now, they had no time.

They were quiet throughout their dinner. Neither had much of an appetite. She could see that it took all his strength just to sit there with her, but he insisted he was fine. He'd wanted to feel normal, sitting there with his wife on their anniversary.

"There is no woman more beautiful than you," he said to her with a soft smile, looking at her across the table and soft candlelight.

Anna shook her head and laughed. She was wearing one of his

favorite dresses, a white sundress with vivid pink flowers and small splashes of blue violets. Her hair was curled and swept on top of her head. She did look lovely. But, no amount of makeup could hide the tension on her face and the dark circles under her eyes that betrayed her own restless slumber.

"It's so unfair Andy," she said after a long pause. "You are the nicest man in the world. Too nice, maybe. I should have gotten this stupid cancer instead. I would have been so furious at it, full of rage. I would have treated it like my personal punching bag. I would have kicked its ass." She caressed his hand across the table.

"That's true. I wished you would have gotten it instead too," he'd signed.

Anna smiled, seeing the teasing in his eyes. She couldn't help but laugh with him. The cancer might be claiming his body but it wasn't crushing his spirit.

"I haven't heard you laugh in a long time," he said carefully as she read his lips. "It reminded me of how long it took me to get you to laugh at me when we first met. You just looked at me with that sarcastic glint in your eyes. I tried all my best jokes on you and failed. It wasn't until I got beat up by a football player and got a bloody, broken nose that you actually laughed at me. Apparently pain has its funny moments. You should be rolling with laughter about now."

"That's not true. I didn't laugh at you that day. I was so mad at that guy," she signed back. Anna struggled to keep the tears from falling. He was such a good man. She had to remind herself constantly that now was not the time to be angry. He needed her love and patience.

"I know you will find a way to enjoy life's funny moments again. That stubborn streak can't be silenced. I know there is irony in that somewhere but the message eludes me," Andy said.

"I'm deaf, remember?"

"Oh, yeah. That," he signed back and chuckled. "If you ask me, that excuse only comes up when it's convenient."

He leaned across the table towards her. "So, you want to fool around, baby?" he said, and gestured towards his hospital bed just a few feet away.

"Always." she signed.

Anna helped Andy to his bed. She retrieved a small gift bag from the floor beside the bed table and handed to him as she climbed onto the bed with him. The two of them lay beside each other, bodies touching and heads together. Anna let herself relax for a moment. He felt so good. His special warmth. She missed him so at night in her lonely bed at home.

She helped him open the decorated bag and handed him the anniversary gift from her. It was a small digital photo player. She turned it on for him and held it for him as they lay there and watched the moments from their lives flash by. The two of them in Anna's dorm room at college, at a basketball game, at Andy's graduation then hers two years later. Their precious wedding pictures and the years of being newlyweds. The pictures of her pregnancy and tiny Allyson being born. Of Allyson growing up and their life as a family.

"I love it. It's perfect," he'd signed. She could see the tears in his eyes and thought that maybe it hadn't been such a good gift after all. She hadn't wanted to make him cry. He noticed her concerned expression and took her hand.

"I know what you are thinking sweetheart, but this is a reminder of what I have been given," he said, "not what I have lost. I am so thankful for each day that I've had with my family and with you, the love of my life, and our precious daughter. Please don't ever forget that I feel this way."

"I'll try not to."

"I love you, princess."

"I love you, my dragon tamer."

Anna watched his face for awhile as he closed his eyes, grimacing in pain. She hated feeling so helpless. Why couldn't she take this sickness from him, fling it away like some blood-sucking leech? She read every single thing about his type of cancer and they tried it all; homeopathic remedies and acupuncture, surgery, dialysis, chemotherapy and radiation. Andy had gone through this plus all the medications and hundreds of hospital trips, yet the cancer hung on.

They would not go down without a fight. However, Andy was slowly, but surely losing the bout.

"Tell me a story," he signed with his eyes still closed, then said out loud. "You know I love your stories. They are always ridiculous and hardly every make a lick of sense. Yet, I am still amazed at the ideas floating around in your head."

"I don't know who enjoyed your 'Glenda and the Three Stoned Bears' stories more, Allyson or I," he continued. "I still don't think that was appropriate story telling for a five year old."

"She didn't know what 'stoned' meant then. She only knew that they talked real slow and ate a whole lot of porridge and potato chips. More than your average bear."

"Tell me."

Anna balled the hand in her lap into a fist, her nails painfully biting into the palm of her hand. She needed to feel that pain to remind herself that Andy needed her and she couldn't break down. She must be the strong one. She would not make his last few months about her pain and sadness.

"There was once a girl named Alice," she said slowly. "She fell down a gopher hole in her backyard...somewhere in Texas." Andy raised one eyebrow skeptically. "She dug and dug and all of a sudden this huge oil gushed out of the ground and flung Alice straight up and up...over the ocean she went, flying past airplanes and cruise ships, past curious whales, topless mermaids and giant sea turtles. All of a sudden, this island came into view and Alice descended so fast toward it that she knocked herself out, landing head first onto a young man looking straight up at her. When she wakes up there is this group of boys, rag tailed and dirty faced and pointing spears right at her. One of them steps toward and demands, "Who are you and why have you killed Peter Pan?"

"That's terrible," Andy signed.

"So, that's the story on how the band 'Alice and the Lost Boys' was formed," she said. Andy laughed out loud, shaking his head. She smiled at his enjoyment. The laughter she couldn't hear but felt in her heart just the same. He kept his eyes closed and she lay there watching him for a long time as he fell asleep with a smile on his thin face, holding her hand in one of his, and the digital player held close to his heart with the other.

***

Anna turned off the digital player and leaned against a box of old Christmas ornaments. In one corner of the dusty room, she noticed a large, old, tin snowman ornament. It's cheerful face with button eyes, black top hat and fake carrot nose looked festive and merry as if just waiting for it to snow so it could break out into a sappy Christmas carol. Anna wanted to punch it in the face.

She heard a sound on the stairs. "Mom? Are you up here? Are you alright?" Allyson called from below. At the sound of her daughter's sweet voice, it took all she had not to burst into tears, yet again.

"Mom?" Allyson called again as she came up the stairs. She saw her mom sitting on the dusty floor, wearing her Dad's old college sweatshirt. She looked lost in it, the worn cotton too big for her small frame. Her face held a look of sorrow that she couldn't hide.

"What are you doing up here?" she asked her.

"I thought I could find something with your Dad's voice on it," Anna told her. "But, so far I haven't found one thing. To be honest, I'm kind of pissed about that."

Allyson sat beside her mother and noticed the digital photo player in her lap. She remembered it well.

"I'm sorry, Mom," Allyson said suddenly. "I'm sorry for all those summers I didn't come home after Dad died. I'm sorry I didn't call you as often as I should have. All those times you invited me to come home for a weekend or to go to dinner and I just made excuses. I'm sorry that I was selfish and thought only of my own loss. Most of all, I'm sorry that it took something as crazy as your disappearance to realize how much our relationship had deteriorated. I'm so thankful I have this chance to tell you now."

Anna looked at her daughter with love in her eyes, seeing her pain. Her heart ached to see Allyson carrying so much grief and guilt!

"I'm sorry too, sweetheart," she told her daughter as she took her hand in her own. "I'm starting to remember those months after your Dad's funeral. I didn't want to talk to people or see their pity. I just wanted to numb myself to the world around me and that included you too, unfortunately. There is no right or wrong way to deal with grief. We each do it in our own way. A lot of times that meant doing whatever it takes to dull the pain. Sometimes we just crawl into a shell of self protection." She shifted on the wooden floor.

"I was so angry, Allyson." she continued. "Angry at everything and everyone. Just like I had been at 16 years old. Your Dad had helped me to look at my life differently. To take that inner strength that I used to keep people at bay and use it to accept myself as a strong, capable woman and to embrace my life. Then he was gone, and the anger came back with a vengeance."

"I found myself sitting in traffic just cursing the other drivers for no particular reason. I even cursed about the weather. No matter the climate, I'd find a way to bitch about it. Even sunny days brought out my scorn and loathing. The neighborhood kids that had always waved at me as they road their bikes down the street now looked at me like I had tentacles growing out the sides of my head. I guess after hearing me scream 'keep your damn toys off my lawn' more than once, will bring that reaction on," she said wryly.

"I was angry at the students that came in the library asking for a reference book and I tried not to look at them with disdain and contempt when they ask me about the mating habits of sea lions and polar bear extinction in the Arctic Circle," Anna shook her head slowly as she continued. "Somewhere people still gave a shit about these things apparently."

"When I would be in line at the grocery store check-out I would have these fantasies about being in the produce department and just standing there in front of a cartful of peaches or oranges or large grapefruit and just going absolutely berserk. Picking this produce up and screaming at the top of my lungs like some suburban Ninja. Grabbing the fruit and throwing it as hard as I could at people as they ran and ducked for cover. Everyone who told me that your Dad was in a better place or it was God's will that he died. All those well meaning people who I smiled politely at for months until my face felt frozen and numb, just beaming them in the back of the head or knees or POW right in the face!"Anna laughed. "It felt so good! I just went through all this fruit like having one of those baseball pitching machines for an arm and literally cleared out the store."

"Do you think that's crazy?" she asked her daughter.

"It's only crazy, if it's not produce," Allyson said as she took her mother's hand and held it in her own. The two laughed together. God, it felt so good to laugh. It was indeed a reminder of what they still had in front of them.

CHAPTER SEVENTEEN

The Indiana Bureau of Investigation sent two agents to interview Anna about her disappearance and return. Sheriff Cole escorted them inside, and Eddie had arrived just a few minutes before they'd gotten there so he could prepare them all for the interview.

"Just tell them what you've already told us, Anna," he told his sister as he watched the three women clean up the breakfast dishes. He had left hours ago, even before sunrise. There was so much to take care of in town with all the crazy reporters and traffic. He'd needed to reschedule Anna's physical exam until after Christmas. She told him that she was ready this time to get it over with. Eddie sure hoped she was right. He wished that it didn't need to be done, but he knew for her sake it was best to get answers and facts if they could. Although facts would probably be a long stretch. Truth and reality seemed to be on a collision course with science fiction.

"I'm ready," Anna said. She seemed much calmer this morning. Her hair was swept up on the top of her head, and she was wearing a bright red sweater and black slacks. She looked lovely, albeit a bit too thin. He had a sense that there were changes about his sister that went way deeper than physical appearance.

Now, the two agents sat at the dining room table. Both wore dark suits, and the younger of the two sat across from Anna. He introduced himself as Agent Robert Timmons and the older one next to him was Agent Gary Young. Sheriff Cole had shaken her hand briefly when he arrived, giving her an encouraging smile and whispering "welcome home," as the four of them found places at the table. Eddie was standing, leaning next to the dining room hall entrance, his arms folded across his chest. Allyson and Jane hovered anxiously in the entranceway from the kitchen.

"Mrs. Anderson, this is a recorded conversation," Agent Timmons told her as he placed a recording device on the table in front of her. "Just start at the beginning about where you were found, if you could, please."

Anna clasped her hands together in front of her. The agents had unreadable expressions. Eddie had told her last night that the IBI and the Sheriff's office already knew about her return and circumstances. They also were told that there were physical changes, including regaining her hearing. As the two men stared at her, Anna wondered if they thought she might be crazy. She was tempted to start laughing hysterically and prove them right. She clasped her hands tighter together and glanced at Sheriff Cole's kind face. She had known him such a long time, most of her life. She would focus on this kindness and not the skepticism she saw lurking under the professional demeanor of the agents.

She took a deep breath and slowly told them how her reappearance had all unfolded. Her appearance on the dark highway outside of Greenway, her stumbling towards town and of Mark Browning finding her leaning against a lamppost.

Anna glanced up at the agents. That was all they needed to know, wasn't it? They both knew the rest from the police reports of the incident. Incident. Again, Anna found herself wanting to burst out laughing. She took a deep, calming breath.

"Mrs. Anderson, what was the last thing you remember before you found yourself standing on the highway on the outskirts of Greenway?" Agent Young asked her in a calm, professional voice.

Anna saw a look of sadness and sorrow cross Allyson's face.

"I remember my husband Andy's funeral."

"Mr. Anderson's funeral was over three years ago, is that

correct?"Agent Timmons asked.

"Three years, one month and eight days ago."

Eddie moved away from the wall and sat down beside his sister. He put his arm around her shoulders and gave it a squeeze. "Let's get this over with as quickly as possible," he said.

"Just following procedure, Chief Monroe," Agent Timmons said with a long look.

Eddie stared back at the agent. What the hell was he getting at? He reminded himself not to let them rile him. They were just doing their job.

"Let's move on." Sheriff Cole said from the doorway.

"You do not remember the day of December 12th at all? Getting up to work and your co-worker Laura Sims picking you up? You do not remember working at the library that morning or being in your sister-in-laws car at noon as she drove down Main Street? You do not remember the accident that took place that day as you sat in the passenger seat of her car?" the agent asked.

"No, I don't remember any of that."

"When you were at the police station on the early morning hours of December 21st, you also came to the realization that you were no longer deaf. Is that correct?"Agent Young asked, a bit more kindly.

"Yes," Anna said softly, looking down at her hands. How could she convince people it was true when she, herself, still had a tough time believing it?

"Do you have any idea how this could happen, Mrs. Anderson? Do you have any idea of where you were for almost nine days?"Agent Young asked her.

"No, I don't," Anna felt Eddie's comforting arm around her and felt yet again, the rock of support that her family was. She hated that she was the cause of all this turmoil.

"It's the craziest thing," she said almost in a whisper. "but, I'm so thankful to be home. To be here with my family. It doesn't matter to me where I was those missing nine days. It doesn't even matter that you believe me or not."

Anna got up from her chair. Everyone was staring at her.

"And frankly, I don't give a damn if you do or not. I think we are done here. Thanks for stopping by, Agent Timmons and Agent Young," she reached across the table and shook hands with two startled agents as each stood up abruptly.

"Merry Christmas, James," she told the Sheriff as she moved away from the table and hugged him briefly. She didn't look at anyone as she crossed the entranceway and went up the stairs, leaving them all standing there staring after her.

***

"Frankly, I don't give a damn?" Eddie said to her after escorting the agents and Sheriff Cole out. Allyson and Jane had followed Anna up the stairs. She was in her bedroom, sitting on the window seat, looking out at the gray, overcast day.

"I always wanted to say that," Anna said. Two red cardinals were flitting back and forth between the tree branches and her depleted rose bushes. She made a mental note to go outside and listen to them sing their sweet twittering melody. It was something she had missed so much.

"Well, I don't think saying it to two Federal Agents was great a great way to do that," Eddie told her, shaking his head.

Anna didn't respond.

"I need to go back to work," Eddie finally said.

Anna turned and looked at her family. They'd been putting their lives on hold for her.

"Go home, Jane," Anna told her sister-in-law kindly. "I know you must have things to take care of. You have a business to run. I appreciate you taking the time to be here and stay with me, I really do."

"Anna, there's nowhere else I'd rather be then here. None of that matters all that much," Jane told her, sitting down next to her on the window seat.

"It alright, Jane. Allyson is here with me. We are quite capable of holding down the fort while the battle rages on the front lines," Anna looked at Eddie. He gave her a withering look in return. "Tomorrow is Christmas Eve. We can get together again then and spend Christmas day together too."

Jane sighed deeply. "Alright," she said. "but I'll be back tomorrow first thing. We will cook and drink and be merry. Maybe even all at the same time. Not one word, mister, about your needing to drink to eat my cooking." She wagged a forefinger at her husband, who threw his hands in the air as to say "who me?"

"We will be back tomorrow, sweetheart," he said. "I'll check all the locks again before I leave. There will be an officer outside all night. The blockade is still up at the street entrance," They hugged each other tightly. "Your neighbors love you, by the way," he said as he pulled away.

"I can only imagine." Anna said with a laugh. "I bet the pitchforks and torches will be coming forthwith as night falls."

Eddie shook his head at her. "You have a crazy imagination, lady!"

"That's a very good thing," Anna told him. How could they have gotten through all this without believing in the impossible, without believing in miracles?

"A very good thing, indeed."

CHAPTER EIGHTEEN

Allyson invited Mark Browning over to have Christmas Eve dinner with the four of them. He had no family there and his father was in Florida. She used this excuse as she told her mom she'd asked him over. Anna smiled at her, trying not to laugh. She was glad for it actually, and looked forward to getting to know Mark better. She was also glad that Allyson had someone special in her life, although Allyson blustered at calling him more than a friend.

Jane brought most of the food over from her house and Anna scraped together ingredients to make Christmas cookies with Allyson. Not being able to go out was starting to take a bit of a toll on them. Anna was thankful she found the Christmas gifts she supposedly bought before the accident in her bedroom closet. She wrapped each gift up with old wrapping paper or colorful bags she found in the attic. It was a strange feeling, not being able to remember buying them. She had to guess which gift was meant for each family member.

At dinnertime Anna watched Allyson and Mark as they talked and laughed in the kitchen. They were making a salad together and teasing each other. Allyson looked beautiful in her green sweater and blue jeans. Her hair, down for once, falling in waves past her shoulders. She was looking shyly up at Mark as he talked to her, their voices too low to be heard.

"What's going on with them?" Eddie asked as he came to stand beside her. He looked more relaxed to Anna, but his eyes were still weary. He was wearing a black button down long sleeve linen shirt and black jeans and sipped his beer straight from the bottle as he continued to watch his lieutenant and niece.

He still needed to talk to Mark about this budding relationship but there was never time. At least Allyson looked happier than she had in weeks. That was the important thing.

"I'm not really sure, Mr. Cash," Anna whispered back at him as she watched her daughter giggle about something Mark said. Apparently making a salad had its hilarious moments.

"Excuse me?" Eddie asked her.

"What? Are you not the man in black?"Anna asked him then started to laugh.

Eddie tried to look at her sternly, but finally gave up attempts to hide his amusement. She always could make him chuckle, even at the expense of his own dignity. There hadn't been a whole lot to laugh about the last few days.

"Very funny, Miss O'Hara," he replied. "Frankly, I don't give a damn what I wear."

"It's a very colorful Christmas attire, dear brother," she told him sweetly ignoring his Gone With The Wind jab.

He tried to glare at her, but again he failed. "At least I'm not wearing some God-awful reindeer sweater like *some* people."

Anna was trying to think of a witty retort that would dignify ugly attire, but the doorbell rang, startling all five of them.

"What the hell?" Eddie said as he put his beer bottle down on the table and went to answer the door. After a few seconds he came back with an amused look on his face and gestured to all of them to come to the front door.

In the front yard stood all the neighbors on her street bundled up in coats and colorful scarves and hats, red cheeked from the cold. They were in four rows, about 35 people altogether, adults and teenagers and young kids. They smiled at the group by the door as they each held cards out in front of themselves with gloved hands.

The young officer that had been standing outside on duty stood with them, hiding his grin with his hand.

Silent Night, Holy night
All is calm, all is bright

Anna listened to their voices as they blended in melodious harmony with each other. The children's sweet voices mingling perfectly with the adults as each voice soared and swayed, lifted and fell in concordant rhythm.

Round yon Virgin, mother and child
Holy infant, so tender and mild

None of them knew how great a gift this was for her. They had no idea yet that she could hear their wonderful voices. These were people she had known for years. Women she had book clubs with and chatted about gardening and recipes and child rearing. Teenagers and children she had known since birth that she'd babysat and Andy had taught in high school. Kind souls who'd brought meals and flowers when Andy was sick. The men who mowed her yard and fixed things around her house without being asked when Andy could no longer do day to day things. They were those that stood up at Andy's memorial service and spoken of him with relevance and fondness and gratitude for his friendship and his gift of teaching. They were the people who had stood beside her in the rain at Andy's casket and gravesite on that dreary November day. They were her friends.

Sleep in heavenly peace
Sleep in heavenly peace.

She had closed herself off to all of them after Andy died. Anna felt tears run down her cheeks as she watched each one of them, so thankful for this moment and the reminder that people still cared.

The song ended with a flourish and they all called out "Merry Christmas!" Anna rushed down the front porch stairs and hugged each one, thanking them profusely as tears continued to run down her face. Allyson, Eddie, Jane and Mark thanked them as well. Even the young police officer wished each one a happy holiday. It was a special moment Anna knew she would never forgot.

***

Early Christmas morning, Allyson shook Anna awake just as she had on this day ever since she was a tiny toddler. Anna opened one bleary eye to find her daughter's smiling face. She'd drunk a bit too much the night before and so had Jane and Eddie. There had been much laughter and celebration and toasting. The three of them had finally ran out of things to be thankful about after Eddie's last toast, "I'm thankful for soft toilet paper" which a slightly tipsy Anna and Jane snorted with laughter at.

Mark and Allyson watched all this with amusement from the den where they had gone to sit and talk quietly to each other as the others made loud chatter in the dining room. Christmas music played on the small stereo that Uncle Eddie had brought over from his house. They had all sang along with gusto, and slightly out of tune. Still, it was so much fun!

"Merry Christmas Mommy!"

"Merry Christmas yourself, Stormy!"

Anna reached out and touched her daughter's face. Allyson looked happier then Anna could remember.

Anna put her arm around Allyson as they went down the stairs in their Christmas nightwear. They walked into the den and Anna plugged in the Christmas tree. She wrapped her arms around Allyson as they stared at the tree.

"Dad loved Christmas. Remember he was sometimes up even before I was?" Allyson said "I miss his cinnamon rolls." Her dad had loved baking rolls. He also loved grilling and barbecuing, but he drew the line at cooking eggs and casseroles and stews and the like. He used to joke that a man who baked mostly desserts had to save his dignity somehow by not resorting to the lesser culinary skills of day to day meals. Allyson smiled at this memory. How she missed him!

Anna tried to remember the last Christmas they had together as a family but even that memory was vague. It had been a quiet holiday, with just the three of them. Eddie and Jane had gone to Florida. She did remember the feeling of false merriment as they'd celebrated the day, trying to ignore the fact that it would be Andy's last Christmas. Now, she wished she had done so much more to make that day full of joy and happiness.

"I'm sorry Mom," Allyson said, as if reading her thoughts.

"Don't be sorry sweetheart. He did love Christmas. I feel him everywhere in this house, especially now. It's going to be a good day. So much to be thankful for."

"Where the hell is the coffee?" Eddie called from behind them. He was wearing gray sweats and his hair stood up in haphazard angles above his ears.

"Merry Christmas, Uncle Eddie," Allyson told him cheerfully. He grunted in return as she hugged him.

"I'll make some," Jane said as she came down the stairs. She looked chipper and merry for someone who had downed several glasses of wine and shots of hard liquor the night before. Her Christmas pajamas, which sported colorful decorated trees on white cotton, peeked out of her stylish red robe. Her short dark hair was brushed and the bruises around her nose and eyes showed much less angry color. Jane had joked only yesterday about the value of quality make-up. Anna smiled at the sight of her sister-in-law. Jane was always such a lady.

"Honey, no," Eddie shook his head and went to sprawl on the love seat in the den, closing his eyes.

"We've been married for 30 years, Edward Monroe. You never complained about my coffee...much," Jane laughed as she watched her husband.

"I've always been honest about your cooking, baby. You always asked me if it was "bad" or "lousy" or even "tolerable". I always said no to all of them. That was the honest truth. It was never bad, lousy or tolerable. It was almost always "terrible". It's the same story of a woman who asks her husband if her pants make her look fat. The honest answer is always "no". That's because the pants do not make her ass look fat. The fat makes her ass look...fat."

Jane glared at him and he opened his eyes, raised an eyebrow and the hint of a smile showed at the edge of his mouth. The three women burst into laughter.

"Too much noise, women!" Eddie complained as he got up from the love seat. "Merry Christmas, baby!" he whispered to Jane as he hugged her.

"Merry Christmas sweetheart," Eddie told Allyson as he hugged her too, kissing the top of her head.

"Honest hangovers. I love that," Anna told him as he gave her a warm hug.

"It's the only time I can get away with it. Merry Christmas, Anna," and he held his sister close, so thankful she was here.

"Oh, I have some good news, everybody," Allyson said shyly. "I checked my exam scores online and well...I passed all of them. I get to graduate in January."

"Allyson! Congratulations! I'm so proud of you," Anna told her. Allyson had worked so hard for her degree, missing all of her freshman year to help with Andy, then having to start it a year later than her class. She had almost caught up by attending classes every summer. She would graduate only seven months later than everyone else in her class.

"Way to go, sweetheart!" Eddie and Jane told her.

Allyson could hear her father in her head telling her how proud of her he was. She was so glad this phase was over. It had been so difficult to concentrate on college and her studies since freshman year, but it was finally done.

What a contrast this day was from the shock and terror she'd felt when her mom disappeared on her birthday. Now, as she looked around at her mother and Aunt and Uncle's happy faces and knew that it was going to be a wonderful Christmas after all.

CHAPTER NINETEEN

Later in the den, they handed out Christmas gifts. Allyson gave her aunt and uncle tickets to an Indiana Pacers basketball game, which they loved. They gave Allyson a mini iPad, which she exclaimed over. Anna had gotten a fancy fishing pole for Eddie. She'd had a heck of a time trying to wrap it, finally just rolling it in enough paper to wrap a small horse in. He loved it anyway, despite having to tear off the yard of paper. Anna got Jane a coffee table book of roses, her favorite flowers. Jane looked at the beautiful pictures with delight.

Anna got Allyson an eBook gift card and a number of smaller gifts, including her favorite perfume and bath gel and body lotion, jeans, socks and another set of Christmas pajamas with funny looking kittens wearing Santa hats. She had also made stockings for each of them, something she did every single year. It was a tradition she'd gotten passed down from her own mother so many years ago.

As Allyson handed her mother her own gift from her, she wished she had taken more time to get something wonderful. Still, the look of joy on Anna's face when she opened up a new set of first edition books by John Steinbeck, her favorite author, gave Allyson a warm feeling of happiness.

"Thanks so much, sweetheart! I'll always treasure them," Anna told her. She had a very old set from when she was in junior high but they were all coming apart now, no longer readable.

"I also got you these," Allyson told her shyly as she handed her Mom another gift. Inside the brightly colored gift bag were four blank journals.

"I think you should start writing down your own stories, Mom," Allyson told her.

Allyson ran her hands across the journals, and remembered that Andy was always telling her she needed to write her stories. She'd told tales to amuse her family and to see where her imagination would take her, but she never ever thought they were great works of literature, a-la John Steinbeck. She had said to Andy that inside every librarian was a frustrated wanna-be writer. She just never believed that she had what it took to be taken seriously as an author. Anna knew how to find answers and do research, but writing down her own stories so that they made actual intellectual sense and reasoning was a mental hurdle that filled her with self-doubt.

But now, it was the time of second chances. It was definitely something she needed to consider.

"You're right Allyson. I think it could be time," she told her daughter.

"Okay, enough of this sentimental sh..stuff," Eddie chuckled as he handed Anna a large box wrapped in bright green paper that featured the Grinch plastered all over it. The wrapping left a lot to be desired. There was tape everywhere and the edges did not quite meet at each corner.

"I see you wrapped this yourself," she said and laughed.

"Of course," he said proudly.

Inside the box was a handheld CD player and music CD's. So many of them! There must have been at least 25. She took each of them out as her family looked on, smiling. The discs featured all the musicians she loved from the 60's and 70's. Elton John, The Carpenters, Creedence Clearwater, The Beatles, Carly Simon, The Temptations and even Elvis. There was even CD's of The Osmond's and Jackson 5 which made Anna laugh out loud. She knew Eddie hated most of that stuff.

Eddie watched his sister with a grin on his face. He'd actually bought her a nice sweater before the accident but after her return, it no longer seemed like a perfect gift. He had gone to a music store outside Indianapolis on a short break a few days ago, dodging reporters and news crews. He'd rushed around the store searching for every performer he could remember his sister listening to as a kid and teenager, throwing CD's in the cart in a hurry to get out of there before the press picked up his whereabouts. The pimply faced teenage clerk had gasped in amazement at the horde of CD's Eddie dumped on the check-out counter.

"Thanks so much, Eddie! It's wonderful!" she told him as she pulled another CD of her favorite classical piano music out and hugged him. He sat on the floor beside her and put his arm around her shoulders.

"Okay, my turn," Jane said smiling at the scene.

Jane handed Anna a gift bag with a theme of beautiful red cardinals playing in a winter wonderland. Jane knew Anna loved these birds.

Inside was a beautiful multi-colored silk scarf. "Oh, it's lovely Jane! Thanks so much," she said as she stood up and hugged her sister-in-law. She wrapped it around her neck, not caring that it looked a bit silly with her snowman pajamas.

Jane reached down under the tree and picked up the last gift. It was a small box decorated in silver and adorned with a small red bow.

"This is also for you, Anna," Jane told her. Anna was puzzled at the look of uncertainty on her sister-in-laws face. Eddie's face was unreadable but he nodded at Jane in encouragement.

Anna slowly unwrapped the silver paper. Inside the box was a blank DVD, the kind you played on the computer.

"Allyson, do you have a laptop?" Jane asked her.

"Mom's laptop is in my room. I'll go get it," Allyson said as she ran up the stairs. Anna was still puzzled by the look on Jane's face.

Was she nervous? She couldn't quite tell.

Allyson hurried back down the stairs carrying the laptop, almost tripping on her bunny slippers. Anna did not remember buying the computer. Was it new?

"It's already connected to the wi-fi and everything. Just turn it on," Allyson told her.

Anna walked into the dining room and carefully set the computer down on the table. She turned it on and the photo of Andy, Allyson and herself at Allyson's high school graduation popped up on the screen.

She sat down on a chair and placed the DVD in the laptop as Allyson, Jane and Eddie stood behind her to watch. As it came alive on the screen, she realized it was Eddie and Jane's wedding video. Jane had transferred it to disk for her.

Anna had seen the video before of course, many years ago on VHS tape. But she'd never heard it. The images of the wedding slowly came to life, Eddie and Jane sitting at the head table and looking beautiful in their wedding clothes, the soft blue colors on the tablecloths and floral pieces, the tables with family and friends surrounding them. The camera panned and Anna watched as her father Bill got up slowly to make his best man speech. Anna gasped out loud. It had been so long since she had heard his gruff, bear of a voice! She blinked back tears as she listened to her beloved father talk about love and commitment and joke about having kids and a mortgage. It was sentimentally sweet.

There were speeches by Jane's cousin who's been the maid of honor and Eddie and Jane both talked as well. And then the disk skipped to a part where she could see members of her family including her mother dancing with Grandpa Wyatt. And, finally there was Anna dancing with Andy. Anna wore her light blue bridesmaids gown and wore her long hair down her back. Andy looked so handsome in his black suit. She closed her eyes against the pain in her chest she felt watching the two of them. They looked so young! They hadn't married yet, but it was clear they were in love.

The camera cut away and people she knew were making speeches to the newlyweds. She laughed at some of her family and friends drunken slurred commentary, and Grandpa Wyatt's short but funny speech. *"Tell each other you love one another every day, no matter how much she annoys you or how much he irritates you enough to want to take a rolling pin to his head,"* he said.

There was her beautiful mother Maria in her lovely dark blue gown. She looked so pretty and happy as she smiled at the camera and simply said, *"Be happy."* Anna felt her heart ache at hearing her sweet voice again and missing her.

Finally the camera panned to Anna and Andy sitting at one of the tables. He was signing to her and Anna leaned closer to the computer screen trying to make out what he said. The camera settled on Anna's up-close face and she said carefully "To Eddie and Jane, I wish you both much love and happiness. If anyone deserves my brother, it is you Jane. Good luck with that." She smiled at the camera and laughed.

Anna heard Allyson, Jane and Eddie chuckling as they peered over her shoulder. And then the camera panned on Andy's face. He smiled at the camera, showing his straight white teeth.

"I wish the two of you the best the world has to offer," he said. His voice was deep and masculine. *"You know what they say about true love. When you find that person you are meant to be with, you do everything in your power to make it happen, even if you have to break down several walls,"* And he turned to look at a young Anna, smiling at him with amusement. Looking back at the camera, straight at a future fifty year old Anna who was listening to his wonderful voice for the first time, his face showed the seriousness she remembered so well when he tried to talk to her about things she didn't want to 'listen' to.

"Most of all I wish you love and happiness no matter what the future holds. Never forget to make each other laugh," he smiled at the camera again. *"No matter what dragons you have to tame."*

That was the end of the disk. Anna sat staring at the screen, grasping her pajama top tightly in her fists, overcome with emotion. Just like it had been with Allyson, Andy had sounded exactly like she thought he would, strong and funny, intelligent and wise. This was the voice she heard in her head and heart throughout their courtship and marriage. It was the voice she knew better than anyone else's. The voice that would stay with her forever.

"Oh, Anna!" Jane said, touching her shoulder. "I didn't want to make you cry, especially today. I wasn't sure if it was the right time to give it to you."

Anna got up from the dining chair and sniffled.

"It was a wonderful, wonderful gift! Thank you so much!" she told her sister-in-law who smiled in relief. Sure, it hurt to watch the disk, but now she had this priceless memento she would watch over and over.

"Merry Christmas!" she told her family as she rushed to pull them into a group hug. It was indeed a wonderful, unforgettable day.

***

At bedtime Anna brought the laptop up to her room and watched the DVD over and over. Each time it got a little less painful to see and listen to.

As she fell asleep she could hear Andy's voice wishing her love and happiness. It had felt like his recorded words had been aimed right at her. It was as though he knew one day she would be watching this video.

That night, *Anna dreamed she was standing on a hilltop, overlooking a beautiful valley. In the distance she could see snow capped mountains and a large body of water. Down the hill was a small city the likes she had never seen. There were men and women wearing brightly colored robes and children, whose robes were all white. The men and women were attending to a large communal garden in the center of the town. They placed what looked to be vegetables into wicker baskets. The children ran along the garden rows, laughing and giggling. Some of the older ones were helping the adults pick the produce. From her perch on the hilltop Anna looked around at the town square. There were no paved streets or vehicles. No cars or buses or trucks. She looked further out and saw a line of igloo-like adobes. Each of them had what appeared to be large solar panels covering the roof and some on the front door as well.*

There were several hundred solar paneled wind turbines in rows along another hillside just outside the town. There were light posts with square solar panels on a smaller scale placed throughout the town along the bricks sidewalks. It was a contrast to both an old and futuristic place. While everything seemed man-made it was also material and design that was not from anything she had ever seen or could recall in her own lifetime.

The town went on for a few miles it seemed. The houses continued on in neat rows. Some of these curious dwellings were larger than the next. She could not see anything that looked like a business or factory. No restaurants or business signs. She saw no electric or telephone poles. The sun was shining brightly overhead and a warm breeze washed over Anna as she stood on the hill looking down on this strange town.

As she turned to look around her, she was startled to find a beautiful woman standing a couple feet behind her.

A much larger dwelling stood in the distance behind this woman, the largest building she had yet seen. Anna was reminded of a museum or large city library. This building had long stone columns like those in Greek Revival architecture. There were rows and rows of stone stairs leading to the large front alcove entrance.

The woman looked at Anna with an air of expectation. Although the woman's long hair was gray, her face was unlined and free of any wrinkles or blemishes. Her eyes were a bright intelligent blue, the coloring oddly familiar. Did she know this woman?

Her facial features were lovely and normal with a small nose and smiling mouth, showing straight white teeth. She looked at Anna with warmth and kindness. She wore a long soft gray robe like the people in the town down the hill. She also wore what appeared to be a pendant of an intricate design around her neck which fell to the middle of her chest. Anna looked at the pendant and felt a prickling of unease, much like she had felt that day at the hospital while she waited to be examined by the doctor. While not fear, it was unsettling.

The woman continued to watch her, and without moving her lips at all said quite clearly in a crisp authoritative voice, "Welcome to our world, Anna."

Anna woke with a start, clutching her blankets to her chest. Her bedside clock showed a time of 12:12 am. It was only a dream, she tried to tell herself, feeling her racing heart. Only a dream.

CHAPTER TWENTY

"I've been thinking that you should move out to the farm, Anna," Eddie told his sister as they sat at the dining table early the next morning drinking coffee. It was still dark outside. The wind had picked up during the night and rain lashed the house in an incessant downpour, battering the windowpanes and roof.

Anna sat at the table holding her warm cup hoping to ease the deep chill she still felt throughout her body. She closed her eyes and listened to the rain hitting the house, enjoying its persistent drumming. While her body still startled in reaction to loud sounds, she was beginning to relax the more she heard. After waking from her dream she'd been unable to go back to sleep. It seemed like it had taken hours for her heart to slow to a steady rhythm. She remembered each unnerving detail of the dream. She kept telling herself that it was only a dream, yet the unease that it brought on was starting to leave her with doubt. Anna was starting to wonder if this "dream" was not a dream at all, but a memory.

"Anna?"

Eddie was holding his own cup of coffee in front of him. He was looking at her with concern.

"Did you sleep?" He asked her. He felt that prickle of unease again when he looked at his sister. There was still so much that bothered him.

"I'm so tired, Eddie. Not just tired, but exhausted by it all. I look at all of you and see that same exhaustion in your faces as well," Anna said as she turned and looked at her brother across the table. "We all have lives, don't we? It's like everything came to a halt as if time came to a standstill." The images of the church marquee and her bedside clock showing the time of 12:12 popped in her head.

"Most of all I'm tired of feeling like a victim. This woman that cries almost all the time and feels afraid and helpless is not me. I've been wondering how I'll ever be able to go back to work at the library. With the media hounding us, that is going to be impossible right now. You and Jane need to get back to your jobs and everyday lives. Allyson will graduate soon and she has a job and an apartment."

"I don't think we can expect our lives to go on like it was," Eddie said. "Look, Anna. None of our lives will ever be the same. Something extraordinary happened to you. I'm just suggesting that you move out to the farm. The property is fenced and away from the road. The entrance is gated and I'll put a padlock on that. Jane and I can move out there with you for awhile."

"No."

Eddie looked at her in vexation. While he was happy to see her stubborn streak return he was not looking forward to an argument with her. He had learned over the long years of being the older sibling that she usually won every argument just by digging her heels in and refusing to listen to his older, wiser counsel. That's the way he saw it anyway.

"I'll consider moving out there but you and Jane are not going to move out there with me. Like I said, Eddie, you need to get on with your everyday lives and this does not include babysitting me. I'm a grown woman, remember?"

"You're just a stubborn little kid in a ponytail," Eddie told her as she glared across the table at him. She did indeed have her hair in a neat ponytail this morning.

"What's this about moving out to the farm?" Allyson asked as she entered the dining room. She looked sleepily at the two of them and yawned. She was wearing her new Christmas pajamas.

Anna glanced at her in amusement. Looking at her daughter in her silly nightwear she was reminded how every Christmas Allyson had gotten new pajamas and that Anna always tried the find the silliest ones for her so that on Christmas morning she could enjoy her daughter's delight over them. Andy had returned the favor by buying her even sillier Christmas sweaters that she wore with pride.

"Your uncle is being his usual snide self by telling me what to do."

Allyson looked between her Mom and uncle, glad to see them getting back to their normal selves. It had been this way for as long as she could remember. The two had always bickered over the silliest things, but Allyson knew how much of that was just good natured teasing. It was good to be home.

"Mom, if you are serious about moving out there then I'll go with you. I'll need time to study for my NCLEX exam and, well, I just want to spend more time with you," Allyson said. She still did not want to let her out of her sight for now. The fear that she had felt when her mother disappeared was still there.

"Sweetheart, you have a part time job at the hospital and an apartment," Anna said. "You all have lives too."

"Mom, you're very much a part of that life!" Allyson said in exasperation. "Besides, I know you don't remember yet but the last three years we haven't spent that much time together. I need to do this. Just for a few months, okay?"

"Alright, just for a few months," Anna said after a long pause. Her daughter could be as stubborn as she was. She got up and wrapped her arms around Allyson and hugged her tight.

"Well, I'm glad I settled that," Eddie said and drank the rest of his coffee, with a smile on his face.

***

At midday, the four of them sat around the dining room to talk about moving Anna and Allyson out to the farm.

"I need to go through all my finances and texts and emails," Anna said. Anna had no idea how much money she had put away. The house was paid for but she remembered Andy's medical bills had been astronomical. Had she make a dent in paying them off in the last three years?

"Eddie, it's time to get the medical exams and tests over with. Also, I'm ready to do an interview and talk about my return and the physical changes," Some of the changes anyway, she thought. "Jane can you help get an interview set up? I'll see if I can get a leave of absence from work. I'm not positive if "extraordinary circumstances" was mentioned in the list of reasons for missing work and paid leave."

Anna stood up from the table. "As my favorite author once wrote 'You're bound to get idears if you go thinkin' about stuff.' Well, I've been thinking that I'm tired of being afraid. I'm tired of being sad. I watched the tape with Andy over and over last night. As I listened to his voice and the words he had chosen I felt somehow he was talking directly to me. It's time to find out what the future holds. It's time to get on with it and slay a few more dragons."

Eddie, Jane and Allyson nodded in agreement. It was time to get on with this business of living.

***

A week later, Anna sat in a chair in the police station interrogation room waiting to be interviewed by Lucille James, a World News This Evening reporter. The days following Christmas had gone by in a blur of medical appointments and reporter assaults happening every time she ventured outside. All of them screamed questions, which upset her. These people still thought she was deaf! She'd kept her head down though she was tempted to turn around and reply to every question just to see how long it would take them to figure out she could hear them. Sometimes people were blind to the obvious.

The four of them had spent a quiet New Years Eve together listening to music and playing board games. Mark Browning had come over to spend time with Allyson. At midnight they all shared a heartfelt toast to the future.

Two days before, Eddie and Jane had gone out to the farmhouse to clean and get it ready to be lived in again. Anna and Allyson had packed their suitcases and boxed up some kitchen and household items to take with them. The Christmas tree and decorations had been put back in the attic. Anna felt a sense of melancholy as she put each ornament back in its packing box. Each one held such a special memory. However, with the same determination she'd felt the day after Christmas, she got it all done quickly and efficiently.

They were escorted out to the farm by Eddie with Mark following in another police car. Jane also followed Mark, driving Anna's car, which had been finally picked up from the shop. She'd filled the backseat with groceries for the two of them. The crush of news vans and reporters also followed but they could not enter the long dirt drive that led to the farm house. The gate was now padlocked and "no trespassing" signs were posted everywhere. Eddie had posted one officer on duty at the gate to keep people away and prevent them from parking on the side of the highway that led up to the entrance. A busier four lane highway was behind the farm house and acreage. Anna and Allyson would have peace and privacy on the farm.

Eddie felt a sense of relief to secure the two women in this safe place. He also knew that Anna knew how to use their Dad Bill's shotgun. Hopefully, it would never need to be used in warning.

Anna had finally tackled her email. She was astounded to find more than 150 texts and over 2000 emails waiting for her to answer. How did all these people get her cell number or email address? So much for privacy rights. She deleted everything that was not from someone she actually knew and told her boss David Harris via text of her need for a leave of absence. He understood completely, and told her she had over three months of paid leave and vacation she could use. Anna was touched by her friends and co-workers best wishes and prayers for her well being. She would miss working at the library, but for the time being, returning to work just wouldn't be possible.

As she sat across from Lucille James, Anna resisted an urge to laugh. Once she revealed that she was no longer deaf, she would put that media attention square on her back all over again. For a moment she was tempted to run away and never discuss it outside her family. But she'd grown so tired of hiding.

She'd agreed to it as a way to pay the money she'd found out she still owed for Andy's illness and as a way, financially, to give herself time to decide what to do with her life. Jane had set up the interview by sorting through all the contact business cards, phone calls and emails she received. Anna had made it clear that this was the only time she was going to discuss her disappearance and return to the media and the broadcasting network was paying her a great deal of money for that distinction.

Earlier Anna and her family had watched Ms. James interviewing Anna's doctors.

Anna had been examined by each of her doctors two days after Christmas at Greenway Community Hospital. Her G.P, dentist and even her ear implant surgeon were astounded, to say the least, about her physical changes. They took x-rays and blood tests and even the DNA test that Eddie thought necessary. Both her dentist and implant surgeon had examined the x-ray results in disbelief.

As Anna listened to their interviews, she felt sympathy as the doctors tried to explain things for which there was no rational answer. Her dentist, Dr. Albert West, kept shaking his head when he talked about her x-rays and the amazing changes. While the shape of her mouth remained the same, no previous dental work or fillings showed up at all. The doctor did not have an answer for it.

The interview with her family physician, Dr. Neil Johnson had been brief. He had only been asked about changes in her physical appearance and he discussed the weight loss and reported that her blood work was "normal". None of the doctors discussed her ability to hear again as they'd decided this would be left to Anna to reveal. Dr. Johnson also stated that the DNA match gave 100% positive evidence that she was indeed Anna Anderson, the mother of Allyson Anderson and sister of Edward Monroe.

It was even more painful for Anna to watch her ear implant surgeon, Dr. Greg Woo talk about the surgery that had not gone as they'd hoped when she was 18. However, working or not, the implant had remained under the skin above her ear ever since.

"Dr. Woo, was there any way at all a surgically implanted device can be removed without further surgery?" Lucille James asked him.

The doctor, retired now, shook his gray-haired head. "It's not something that can just fall out," he'd said with a good-humored chuckle.

"When you looked the x-rays of Anna Anderson's taken days ago, did it seem to you that you were looking at the x-ray's of someone else?" she'd asked, then shown him images on a large screen of Anna's head x-rays from both 1980 and 2012.

The doctor had shifted uncomfortably. He examined the two x-rays. One showed the implant very clearly.

"It did not seem to me that it was someone else's x-ray," he said finally. "I know they came from the same patient. I just can't explain why or how the implant is now missing."

"Hopefully we can find out that answer, doctor," Lucille James said and smiled at Dr. Woo. She shook his hand then looked straight at Anna sitting off camera.

For a moment Anna wondered if she'd made a mistake in agreeing to the interview. Ms. James had seemed kind and professional when they'd briefly talked earlier. She assured Anna that she would make the interview as easy as possible for her. But now, there was a glint of determination in the reporter's eyes.

A sense of uneasiness grew in Anna's stomach. It was too late to back out now. This reporter was on a quest for the truth. The story of her mysterious disappearance and reappearance that had enthralled a nation for over two weeks was about to get even more interesting.

How could Lucille James find out the "truth" about Anna's disappearance when Anna herself still didn't remember? Anna felt Allyson's hand give hers a gentle squeeze.

It was her own turn now.

CHAPTER TWENTY ONE

As Anna sat opposite Lucille James she wound her hands together, willing her tense body to relax. Her crisp black suit and indigo blue silk blouse looked impeccable on her slim figure. She wore the colorful silk scarf that she had gotten from Jane for Christmas, draped casually around her neck and off her shoulder. She had gained a bit of the weight she'd lost in her disappearance back in the last week and she was glad that the suit did not hang on her. Jane had come to the farm that morning to do her make-up and hair. Anna hated all the fuss but now as she sat across the professionally groomed reporter in her expensive suit and designer haircut, she was glad she looked her best.

Before Anna sat down to be interviewed, Lucille James had summarized for the camera Anna's story. She had also briefly touched on Anna's deafness and widowhood.

When she addressed Anna, her voice was slow and careful. "Anna," she said, "the world has been enthralled by your mysterious disappearance and reappearance in this small farming community outside Indianapolis. I'd like to go back to December 12th and talk about the events of that day." She nodded at Anna to go ahead.

Anna took a deep breath and squared her shoulders. "December 12th was my 50th birthday," she started, her voice just above a whisper. She noticed the reporter's slight frown as she leaned forward to listen. Off camera, Eddie gave her a nod and a smile of encouragement.

"I still do not have any memory of that date. I have been told about the events that occurred that day from others. A co-worker of the Greenway Public Library where I work apparently picked me up that morning at 8 am because my car was in the shop," Anna said, this time her voice steadier and calmer as she spoke each word and repeated the events of the day.

When she finished, Lucille James had a skeptical look on her pretty face. "This is where it gets intriguing, Mrs. Anderson" she said. "As police reports and witnesses have all stated in detail, you were not inside this car when these witnesses and emergency personnel approached the damaged vehicle after it was hit. Only your sister-in-law Jane Monroe was inside, unconscious." She stared at Anna as though waiting for an explanation.

Anna looked back at her calmly. What could she say to that? She still didn't remember the day of the accident. So that's what she told her.

"What's the last thing you do remember?" the reporter shot back.

Anna sighed. "I remember my husband Andy's funeral and the months afterwards."

"You husband Andrew died of cancer in 2009," she said. "You do not have any memory of the last three years?"

"I don't remember a whole lot of it," Anna said looking down at her clasped hands.

The reporter shook her head. "I'm not a doctor or medical expert but that sounds like selective memory to me, Mrs. Anderson, don't you agree?"

"I agree that you are no expert, Ms. James."

Lucille James continued to regard Anna steadily as Anna stared back at her defensively.

"Let's talk about the timing. You disappeared on December 12th, 2012 at exactly 12:12 pm. According to police reports again, you reappeared on a highway just outside town on December 21st, 2012 at 12:12 am, almost nine days later. Those numbers are a great curiosity, don't you think?"

"Yes, they are interesting," Anna said carefully. She was not going to allow this woman to bait her. "I'd rather believe that they are meaningful coincidences."

"Meaningful coincidences or science fiction?" Lucille James gave a short laugh and when she did not get a reaction out of Anna her face turned somber. "As a reporter I am very interested in the details of this story. The precise timing is perplexing as well as of course, where you were during those nine missing days. Do you have any memory of those missing days Mrs. Anderson?"

Anna remembered her dream from Christmas night and the vivid details of the images in the strange town, including the gray haired lady that Anna felt such a strong connection to. She had not dreamed it again since and she was not going to tell anyone about this dream yet, least of all this reporter.

"No, I don't."

"Let's discuss your physical changes since your return on December 21st," the reporter continued, looking down at her notes in her lap. "What were some of the differences in your appearance that you first noticed?"

"I noticed that my clothes were hanging on my body a bit as if I had lost weight. I noticed that the implant that has been above my left ear since I was 18 years old was missing. Later on I also noticed the dental work I've had done throughout my adulthood was missing and my teeth seemed perfect. I also noticed that I no longer needed my prescription glasses. However, none of that was the biggest change I noticed in myself," Anna stated.

"What was the biggest change you noticed Mrs. Anderson?" the reporter asked, looking puzzled. She was aware of physical changes Anna had just mentioned and didn't know there'd been others.

Anna looked down at her clasped hands again and took another deep breath. She hoped she wouldn't wish afterwards that she could go back in time and say nothing at all. She looked up at Lucille James waiting eagerly for her response, then at her family on the sidelines. She was afraid that any moment she would let all the buried emotions rise to the surface and flood her heart and soul in a riptide that would overwhelm her ability to carry on a coherent conversation.

"I noticed that I was no longer deaf."

Anna heard the cameramen gasp. Lucille James' mouth had opened in an "O" of surprise. She seemed to be struggling to form a reply.

"Are you stating you've been able to hear since your return on December 21st? That you have been able to hear me this whole interview?" the reporter finally said, in a tone of astonishment that bordered on anger. She apparently did not like being caught off guard.

Anna resisted the urge to chuckle. She was aware of how absurd her statement sounded. An image popped into her head of the skeptical way Andy looked at her as she related one of her ridiculous adventure stories. Anna dared not look at her family because she was afraid their faces might show amusement.

"Yes," she said calmly.

"Well," the reporter said. "That's quite the miracle, wouldn't you say Mrs. Anderson? The weight loss and teeth and eyesight changes are certainly intriguing. The ear implant missing even more so. However this...no longer being deaf, is astonishing."

Lucille James nodded at Anna, waiting for her to go on. Anna stayed silent. She knew that this woman did not get where she was by being passive.

"Would you say that all of this...both your disappearance during what could have been a very tragic event and your reappearance and the changes in you are a bona fide miracle from God?"

Anna should have been prepared for the question, yet she was still surprised by it.

"A woman disappears in the middle of a car accident," Anna told her. "No one can find her or explain why or how it happened. She returns with no idea where she has been. The physical changes in her are incredible. All of that sounds like a miracle to me."

"A miracle directly from God?"

Anna shook her head slightly. She knew she was treading on uncertain ground. She had attended the First Baptist church with Andy where his father was the pastor. They had continued going there as a family even after his father's death. In all that time she never questioned her faith and belief in God. It was only during the time when she realized Andy was going to die had that faith wavered. She remembered praying for a miracle every single day while she nursed her husband dying of cancer.

"I believe that there are a lot of miracles that can be attributed directly and or indirectly to God. Indirectly perhaps through a doctor or medicine or acceptance towards something or someone," Anna told her. "It certainly was a miracle to me to hear my daughter for the very first time."

She glanced at her daughter, who's head was on Eddies shoulder. She could see that she was struggling to hold back her tears. Anna felt her own eyes tearing up at the sight, but she looked back at the reporter with defiance. She would not allow herself to get in a debate about faith and religion, especially when so much of what she felt inside left her uncertain.

"I'm not sure that answers my question," the reporter said. "Do you really want me to end this interview with you stating that with all that happened to you, including regaining your ability to hear again is a miracle, yet you are not certain that miracle came from God?"

"I didn't say it wasn't a miracle from God. I said that I believe it could have came indirectly."

"If this miracle didn't come from God directly or not, Mrs. Anderson, where did it come from?"

Anna struggled to form a reply. She didn't know how to answer the question.

"One last question, Anna," the reporter said. "Why you?"

Why her? Why had this miracle happened to her? Anna thought of this question over and over in her mind for hours each day she'd returned. What was so special about her? There were too many others more deserving, certainly. Families devastated by cancer or unforeseen tragedies, parents losing a child. Even her beloved Andy, certainly deserved this miracle much more than she did.

Anna glanced at her family. "I wish I knew that answer," she said, her voice full of quavering emotion.

Lucille James signaled to the cameramen to stop then gave Anna a long calculating look. "I'll get back to you later if I need to," she got abruptly and moved off camera. Anna could hear her tell one of her assistants to "get Dr. Woo back to go over the hearing loss and get the results of her hearing tests before and after."

They had been prepared for that and Anna had already taken that test as well. Going over the test with the audiologist had actually been a wonderful moment for Anna. The changes in her hearing ability had been astonishing. It was undeniable written proof of what had happened to her.

Anna got up from the chair. The interview could have gone worse, she supposed, but she felt drained both physically and emotionally.

Her family was interviewed later that afternoon. This time Lucille James knew Anna was no longer deaf and she played on the emotions of each one. Anna's heart ached listening to both Jane and Allyson talk about her disappearance and how frantic they had been as well as their joy at her reappearance and astonishment at her physical changes. She felt tears roll freely as she listened to her daughter's voice break when she talked about the early morning hours of December 21st when she found out her mother was able to hear her.

When the reporter questioned Eddie about his involvement in the investigation of Anna's disappearance, he'd answered her in a cool professional manner. Only when he talked about her return had his voice wavered.

"Chief Monroe, let me ask you this. Your sister, Anna Anderson, returns after nine days missing under disturbing circumstances. She not only returns, but returns in a mysterious way, and with incredible physical changes that cannot be logically explained," she leaned in closer to Eddie as he watched her dispassionately. "Is it at all possible that perhaps this woman who showed up on December 21st at 12:12 am outside of Greenway, Indiana is not your sister Anna Anderson? Is it possible, Chief Monroe, that she is someone else altogether?"

Eddie knew this question was coming. He had felt it in his gut all along that one day it would be brought up.

"No," he said firmly. "You saw the DNA report, Ms. James. The test confirmed 100 percent that she is Anna Anderson."

The reporter shifted in her chair and gazed at Eddie with a challenging smile. "I wonder why you felt the need to order this test, Chief Monroe. If you were so certain this woman was your sister, why would you need a DNA test to confirm it?"

"Perhaps because I knew this question would come up from someone like you," he said tersely.

Lucille James looked back at him smugly. She had done her job, all right. She had put the doubt out there that would allow every single reporter and news station, every tabloid reporter and talk show host, to begin to seriously question his sister's reappearance. The DNA test would not stop them from speculating that it wasn't Anna Anderson that had returned, but someone else.

CHAPTER TWENTY TWO

Anna dreamed again that night she was standing on the hilltop overlooking the strange and beautiful town. She watched the people in their colorful robes and the happy children running to and fro in the green grass and garden area below. It was all so peaceful. Anna wanted to run down the hill and talk to them. She wanted to play and laugh with these children. Their exuberance and joy felt so contagious. Anna smiled as she continued to watch them. How wonderful it would feel to be that innocent again.

"These children are our future."

Anna turned to look at the lovely gray haired lady standing beside her.

"Is this heaven?" Anna asked her without moving her mouth.

The gray haired lady smiled back at Anna gently then turned to look back at the people below. "I guess it depends on ones perception of the meaning of 'heaven'. If you mean a place or feeling of supreme happiness or euphoria, perhaps it is," she said and chuckled. "This is our own version of paradise."

Anna looked out over the tranquil valley below and the surrounding mountains and the gulf leading to the huge body of water that spread out as far as the eye could see. If she could describe a vision of utopia, this place would be it.

"So much of what you see in this area is still unspoiled," she

continued as she looked out at the land surrounding them. "In time, that may all change. Despite the intentions of all of our descendants here and those who will come after, we know that it is our nature to create, to build and to explore. We also know it is in our nature to destroy."

She turned to look at Anna and the sadness in her blue eyes gave her a feeling of overwhelming melancholy. This beautiful place destroyed? She had an image of these happy children living in squalor and poverty, tears running in jagged rivets down their dirty faces. Their cries of hunger ignored by those that passed them by. No!

"We can't let that happen," Anna said. Surely, things would be different here.

"Our ancestors came from a world that was much like this one. In the beginning, there was a paradise much like what you see here. The more populated that world became, the more that these people wanted to claim the land solely for their own. They wanted to build and explore and conquer. They built on land soaked with the blood of those they killed for opportunity and in the name of industrial enterprise and global commerce and personal wealth. The wars came and more people died for greed and the inability to accept the differences in each other. The land was raped and the air, soil and water became polluted and rotten. This world became a place of darkness and desolation," the gray haired lady paused and gazed towards the mountains in the distance.

Anna's sudden disquiet had grown into fear as she listened to this woman talk. The happiness she had felt when she found herself standing on the hill overlooking this peaceful valley changed into a sense of foreboding.

The woman looked directly at Anna. "Our ancestors were on the last shuttle out of this dying world less than a thousand years ago. The ship was full of scientists, doctors and teachers and their families. People who all had a vision of a new life and a new world full of promise and peace," she paused. "Everything you see here is man-made. Our homes are warmed by the sun, our food is grown as a community and attended and shared by everyone. Nothing has monetary value. All the illnesses and diseases that people once had in this other world do not exist here. Our medical technology is the best there will ever be. We all had a vision of a world that gave us hope and we set out to make it happen."

Anna felt confusion. This woman was talking about a different world.

"Where am I?"Anna asked. She could hear the apprehension in her own voice.

"The question my dear Anna, is not where you are but where did you come from?"

"I don't understand."

"They came on the last shuttle out from a world that was burning with the fires of war and destruction. A world that was destroyed by human greed and the rapacious need to possess. A world that is now dark and desolate, it's ashes long cooled."

Anna felt her body begin to tremor. She had never felt so afraid.

"It's a world Anna, where humankind no longer exist," the woman paused and looked intently at her. "It's your world Anna. This place called Earth."

Anna awakened from the dream with a violent start. Her face and nightshirt were drenched in sweat. She put her arms across her chest, trying to get the body spasms under control. She glanced at her bedside clock even though she knew what time it was going to show. 12:12 a.m.

***

Allyson sat in the passenger seat beside Mark as they drove back from Indiana Mid-western University campus and her apartment. He'd helped her to gather her things from her rented room. Her clothes and a few house-wares, books and her computer was all that she was taking out to the farmhouse. She felt sad as she stood outside the Victorian home, its faded turrets shadowed in the rain. She had enjoyed her time there, but it was time to move on.

Allyson had been concerned about her mother that morning. As Allyson prepared to leave, she'd seemed upset. Allyson had fussed over her but Anna had shooed her off and said she was fine. It would take time to get used to sleeping in these other beds at the farm, was all Anna would say. It was true that the beds were old and the mattresses lumpy. The house had been cleaned top-to-bottom, but still felt old and unlived in. There was a musty smell that permeated the air, no matter how much air freshener their used. Allyson herself spent a few sleepless nights there since they'd moved in.

They'd left just before their interview had been broadcast two weeks before. They'd been pretty much isolated in the farmhouse ever since. Eddie, Jane and Mark had told her that the news had sent the media into an even bigger frenzy. The news traffic had almost brought the small town to a standstill. Vans filled with cameramen and reporters traveled up and down the highway in front of the road leading to the farmhouse, daily, hoping to catch a glimpse of family members.

Both Allyson and Anna avoided turning on the television at the farm. It took everything the local police had and more volunteers from other counties to regain a measure of control. Her Uncle Eddie and Mark had been working around the clock the last two weeks to try and settle disputes and complaints brought about solely from the media attention and the interview.

Somehow reporters had gotten all their phone numbers. And each time they got a new number, the calls would start all over again. Anna had gotten so angry about the harassment that she had taken her cell phone outside and smashed it with a hammer, then buried in the backyard. Allyson wasn't sure why her Mom felt the need to bury it but she had laughed when Anna finished shoveling dirt over the last broken piece and mockingly saluted it.

She and Mark had been followed partway to the college but he finally lost most of the news vans on the state highway that ran alongside the school. Allyson glanced at Mark as he drove his car along the rain drenched highway. He was such a sweet guy, she thought to herself. She had never felt this way about anyone and in such a short amount of time too. All these new feelings she had for him, made her nervous as heck. She felt like she was in a constant state of intense emotion every time she was around him. She laughed to herself, remembering how so many times she told her friends that she wasn't going to fall in love for a long, long time, maybe never. However, falling in love she was. Their first kiss on Christmas Eve as they stood outside saying good night had sealed her fate. She was starting to believe that she maybe could have that great love that people talked and wrote songs about, as silly as it sounded. That incredible love her parents had had for each other.

"So, young lady, how are you, really?" Mark asked her in a teasing voice as she looked out the window.

It was gloomy outside but as she turned to look into his kind brown eyes she felt the warmth of a beautiful sunny day. He reached out and touched her hair as they waited at a stop light.

"I know you don't want to hear "I'm OK" again," she said to him. "My Mom and I get up each day and make small talk and we go about our day. We clean the farmhouse and walk the fields when it's sunny out. She talks about my grandparents and great-grandparents and their lives and history out here. She plays the old piano in the den that she played as a child. I love seeing her enjoyment over hearing again. Her music seems to give her peace. I watch as she sits outside all bundled up and listens to the birds on the patio. I don't have words to explain the expression on her face as she closes her eyes and listens to their sweet songs."

Mark took her hand and held it in his big warm one. He was failing in love with this beautiful girl quickly, surprising himself. It really had been so simple and easy.

"We never talk about it, you know, the accident and her disappearance," Allyson said as Mark caressed her hand with his. "It's the proverbial elephant in the room. Uncle Eddie will sometimes ask her if she remembers anything at all but she always has the same answer. No. I have told her that if she ever wants to talk about it, I'm always there to listen to her, but she keeps saying she remembers nothing. I really don't know if there will ever be an answer to it at all."

"There could be, Allyson. Perhaps one day. Sometimes we remember what we wish to. Maybe she doesn't want to remember," Mark said.

Allyson nodded in agreement.

"I need to stop and get gas. Do you want some terrible gas station coffee?" Mark asked.

"Only if you buy me some terrible gas station donuts as well," she said and smiled back at him.

Mark pulled into a Speedy gas station. Allyson stretched and got out, happy to be outside even if it was raining. She waved at Mark and ran inside, shaking the wet drops from her jacket. She got two cups of coffee for them and the donuts. God, she was acting silly. It was raining and cold and she was standing in a dirty gas station buying junk food yet she felt a glimmer of happiness. Allyson took her loot up to the cashier. Beside the cash register was a magazine rack. Every one of the newspapers and tabloids it held featured a story about her mother.

She read the headlines with a feeling of rising nausea. "ANNA ANDERSON WAS CLONED", "ANNA ANDERSON ABDUCTED BY ALIENS", "ANNA ANDERSON'S 'MIRACLE' NOT FROM GOD", "MISSING WOMAN IS NOT ANNA ANDERSON."

"That will be $4.60, miss," the cashier said but Allyson didn't hear him.

"Ma'am?" he asked again.

"Allyson? It's okay, sweetheart. Let's go," Mark said as he glanced at the newspapers then threw a $20 on the counter for the gas but left the coffee and donuts. They got in the car and he pulled it into a parking space facing the highway. Allyson's face had become pale as ice.

"Baby, don't worry about what those jackals wrote," Mark said, pulling her into his arms. "They don't know anything. They're just making up shit because they can't get any information," What words could he say to comfort her? As a police officer he had spent so many hours going over Anna's accident and disappearance and her reappearance but hadn't come up with any answer that made sense. He wasn't surprised at the tabloid headlines.

Mark's words didn't help the fury Allyson was feeling. These people knew nothing! She pulled away from him, jumped out of the car and stormed across the pavement into the gas station. She could hear Mark calling after her.

Inside, she grabbed all the newspapers and magazines from the rack and threw them on the counter at the startled cashier.

"Put all this bullshit on my card!" she screamed at the open mouth teenager as he looked on in alarm.

"Uhm, uh, cash or credit miss?" the cashier choked out as he started to ring them up.

"For god-sakes! Credit! Hurry up!" she yelled at him. Mark came through the door and stood behind her quietly. The cashier rang up the total and Allyson angrily signed the receipt. She and Mark gathered up the papers and headed back to the car.

Along the way, Allyson noticed some of the other customers were staring at her. "What the hell is the matter with you all? Haven't you ever seen a person go berserk in a gas station before?" she said.

"The damn gas prices are going up again," Mark told them as he followed Allyson to his car.

He opened the door and got in the driver's seat and looked at Allyson while he tossed his own papers into the back. She was shaking with emotion.

"So, what's the plan now?" he said. "If you want, we'll hit the gas station across the street and the two on the next corner and every grocery and drugstore between here and home and we'll buy every piece of bullshit that we can find. You can use both my credit and debit cards and hell, even my gas station card if that helps."

Allyson didn't know if she wanted to laugh or cry hysterically, but, she did neither. She just sat there dejectedly. They could never buy all these trashy stories. It wasn't going to change a thing. All she could do was try and protect her mother from them.

"I'm beginning to see why Eddie calls you 'Stormy'. In fact, I'm pretty darn turned on," Mark told her as he pulled her to him.

"You're crazy," Allyson said.

"What? I'm crazy?! The lady who went 'berserk' in a gas station is calling *me* crazy?" Mark shook his head.

"Maybe I am crazy," he said as he pulled her gently away so he could see her face. "Crazy about you."

Allyson felt her breath leave her body for an instant and looked at him tearfully and smiled.

"You're the bravest person I have ever met Allyson. No matter what happens from here on out, I'll be beside you. We will get through all of this together," he told her and gently cupped her face and kissed her.

CHAPTER TWENTY THREE

Anna sat on the back patio of the farmhouse. The air was so cold she could see her breath. But it was mid-February and the sun was shining and she felt the need to be outside. She came out often to just sit and listen to the sounds that had become an important part of her life. She listened to the birds and the sound the wind made as it whooshed past the house and through the open fields. She listened to the far away sounds of the cars and trucks on the highway beyond the property and once in awhile the bark of a dog or the moo of a cow. But she rarely heard the sound of human voice this far out.

Whenever she thought back to her interview with Lucille James, she wished she could have clarified her belief in miracles and that this all was indeed a gift from God. What did it matter if this miracle came directly or not? Perhaps it wasn't meant to be understood, only cherished.

It was strange, she could hear again, yet both the past and current circumstances and not being able to share so much about these feelings with her family, were taking a toll on her. Even surrounded by people and sounds, she felt an ache of loneliness.

Anna thought about her new neighbor as she took her morning walk. Eddie had told her the little bit he knew about the man who lived to the west of them. That Mr. Alexander was a college professor or something and taught agriculture was basically all he knew.

Anna had stood rooted to the spot as Mr. Alexander hailed her from the other side of the barbed-wire fence that separated their properties. Of course, she had bolted like a startled deer. She was still not used to being around people other than her own family. She still couldn't get past the feeling that everyone out there must think she was some kind of freak.

She picked up her mug and took a sip of hot tea, staring at the red barn. The barn really needed to be painted again she thought, as her eyes ran over its weathered features. It had been standing for close to 75 years or so, replacing the original one that was destroyed in a violent thunderstorm when her parents were newly married.

Living in this house again brought back so many memories of growing up here. She felt closer to both her parents and grandparents as she walked the rooms, so conscious of the house's history. Her mother had walked these same floors when she and Eddie had been babies and on nights they'd been sick. Her father had paced the same floors when he worried about the farm or money or some impending catastrophe.

She'd retrieved all the old photo albums her parents and grandparents had accumulated over the years from the attic and placed them on the worn coffee table in the living room. She looked at all of them with Allyson, telling her daughter the family history again. Allyson had heard the family stories a few times in her life but it had been a long time since they talked about it, long before both of her grandparents had passed away.

The old upright piano in the living room had been in their family for three generations. It originally belonged to her Grandma Wyatt then passed down to Anna's mother, then to her. Grandpa Wyatt had relished telling the story about trading two barrels of good, old-fashioned corn liquor for the piano, a gift to his new bride. "Best deal I ever made," he had said, winking at his wife.

Eddie tuned the piano for her, grumbling that it should be used for firewood as he sucked a splinter he'd gotten from the worn wood out of his hand. However, when he listened to her play, it was hard for him not to show how emotional it was to hear her playing her beloved music again.

The first night back in this house had been difficult for Anna. Memories of her parents tore at her already vulnerable heart. As she stood in the doorway of the old-fashioned bathroom, she vividly remembered being 16 years old and violently ill, laying her feverish body on the cold floor. The next thing she knew, she was waking up in the hospital and no longer able to hear.

As she sat outside in the cold air, she thought about her recent dream once more. The feeling she'd had as she had stood on that hill overlooking that futuristic valley had been so similar to waking up from the hospital that day more than 34 years ago and realizing her world had changed. When she stood on that hill, as though awaking from a dream, she could hear all the sounds of that valley and even though the gray haired lady had spoken without moving her mouth, she clearly understood everything she said to her.

"Our medical technology is the best there will ever be," was one of those things.

Did that have something to do with regaining her hearing, or was it just a dream?

She still couldn't process what the older lady had said to her about Earth's apocalyptic future. Why had she told Anna this? What could *she* possible do to prevent such a catastrophe from happening? She was just a small town librarian. She had no intention of going out in public again and telling the world anything more about her life and these visions. She wished she could go back to this strange world and tell the gray-haired lady that she made a mistake, that Anna wasn't the person who could save her own world. She couldn't even talk to one neighbor without bolting. No, Anna wasn't any kind of hero. She took another sip of her now lukewarm tea and felt that these dreams were not over. Perhaps, they were just beginning.

***

Eric Alexander took a walk through the saturated cornfields of his farm. His muddy black rain boots made squishing noises as he moved from depleted row to row, visualizing the planting he would do in the Spring. His warm brown coat kept the morning chill at bay as he walked the acreage that bordered the Monroe farm.

He was a tall man at 6'2". His lean frame made a slim silhouette as he continued walking across the fields. His bright blue eyes shown with intelligence, the smile lines attesting to the humor he found in life and the pleasure he received from laughing often. His hair, once blonde, was mostly gray now but full and thick just as it had always been most of his 54 years. The lines on his handsome face bore testament to a life spent predominately outdoors.

He'd purchased this small 90 acre farm just two years before. There was still much to be done here but he had a vision of a solar energized, completely organic, wind powered working farm in the near future. A teacher of Environmental Studies and Agriculture Science at the community college in nearby Brownsboro, each spring he brought some of his students out to the farm for research on the soil, water and plants. They discussed the potential for solar energy, greenhouse heating and wind turbines on his farm as well as pest management and alternatives in crop planting and hydroponics. Eric planted mostly corn and wheat and he had a small crop of soybeans each year. He also attended to his own vegetable garden and the farm had about 50 apple trees but they needed a lot of work before they would become a part of cash crop again He hoped that even after he retired as an educator that the agricultural students would continue to use his farm for studies.

He was originally from upstate New York. He had been an only child of two loving parents who also had been teachers. Both of them has passed away many years ago. Eric had grown up in the eastern part of the state near Lake Erie. He spent his childhood swimming, boating and sailing its shores. Strange, that here he was in Indiana being a farmer, he thought and chuckled to himself as he neared the fence in his property that separated it from the farm that was directly east of his. While he loved the water he also loved the soil. As far back as he could remember he had been fascinated by how plants grew. Many of his school science projects had been about seed germination and the biodiversity of insects in his back yard. He remembered the year in 6th grade when he had raised his own lady bug farm for plant research and accidently knocked over their container and released more than a hundred on them into his house. Both his parents had looked on nonchalantly as each tiny bug made its presence known in the house on the furniture, household plants, in closets and window sills. He was never sure if he had caught them all. One seemed to show up every once in awhile, perching on top of his Mother's hair or his Dad's pipe. His Dad would only say "thank goodness he's an only child" and wink at his Mother.

Eric had gotten a job at the Brownsboro college a few years ago. First he had lived in a small apartment until he was ready to buy the thing he truly wanted most of his life, a small farm. He'd married his college sweetheart Jennifer Tate in 1983 and had gotten a job at a large chemical manufacturing company where he worked on the development of new products. It certainly was not his goal in life but starting out as a married man, the money was good. However, as the years passed he became more and more discontent with his life. Jennifer had not understood his passion for plants and gardening and his yearning to be a teacher. She had dismissed any ideas about them living on a farm. Their marriage slowly came apart and they divorced in 2003. Eric was deeply saddened at the time about his marriage ending but he knew it had been for the best for both of them.

He could see the Monroe's red barn and the white farmhouse far in the distance. Now, there was a curious story he thought to himself. Eric had met Eddie Monroe, Greenway's Chief of police a few times in passing. He knew that the Monroe's had not lived on their place for some time but the acreage was still farmed to pay for the upkeep of the property. Their farm was more than three times the size of his and he was a bit envious. It would be hard work, but wonderful to have so many possibilities cultivating that amount of land.

Eric stood staring across the property lines and thought about the story of Anna Monroe Anderson. He'd seen her walking the land a few times and had waved at her once but she'd stared at him like he was a poacher caught stealing a chicken and bolted across the frozen fields back to her house.

When he first read about her disappearance in the local newspaper the whole thing seemed so extraordinary yet improbable. If he hadn't had a Christmas tree sitting in his living room as he read the paper he would have checked his calendar to see if it was April Fool's Day. How was it even possible that someone could disappear like that? The paper portrayed her as a grieving widow. For those days she was missing, Eric had actually believed that Anna Anderson had just walked away from all of her pain. Then, she mysteriously returned and those thoughts were tossed out the window. But he'd remained skeptical even when he was battling some news van for a parking space downtown or cursing being stuck in media traffic for miles all around Greenway. It was indeed the craziest story he had ever heard yet it was the only thing everyone in town, heck in four counties, was talking about. A lot of people sure believed it.

His opinion about Anna Anderson had changed from skepticism to compassion when he watched the World News This Evening interview she'd done with Lucille James a few weeks ago. He remembered her careful speech and the way the light caught her pale face and blonde hair. She seemed so earnest and honest. When she had dropped the bombshell about not being deaf any longer, there had been a slight lift to her mouth as though revealing this particular secret amused her. The look on the reporters face made Eric laugh out loud. As he saw how defensive Anna had gotten at the verbal assault of questions that came after, he felt sympathy rise up for her. She was clearly trying to give honest answers to things she obviously did not yet understand.

He was a man of science. He performed research toward a comprehensive understanding of nature and the environment. What happened to Anna Anderson was so far out there, the events so illogical, that he wished he could talk to her and find a way to help her understand it. As he listened to her struggle over trying to explain the word 'miracle', there was something in her blue eyes that touched him. It was indeed an incredible story.

CHAPTER TWENTY FOUR

Spring finally came to Indiana. The cold dreary days gave way to sunshine and warm breezes. In early May, Anna sat atop "Tillie," her dad's tractor, which was towing the planter that was laying the soybean seed in a precise manner along even rows. She was wearing an old blue t-shirt and worn jeans. Her blonde hair was in a pony tail and on her head was her father's faded 'John Deere' cap.

The soil had already been tilled for planting a few weeks before. Robbie Miller, her neighbor, had planted and harvested the crops for the Monroe family farm every year since her father Bill had retired. He would plant the bigger crops of corn and hay for them, but Anna wanted to become more involved in the planting season.

Surprising herself and her family, it was Anna who carried the Monroe family farming tradition in her blood.

"You have the dirt in the blood little sister. I expect corn to start sprouting out of your ears by next Spring," Eddie told her one day, teasing her.

She drove the old tractor at a slow pace, enjoying being outside in the warm weather and listening to the sounds the old tractor made. Anna had learned to drive a tractor in her early teens, but she had never planted crops.

Anna eyed the worn and faded decal above the driver's side door of a very buxom blonde woman from the 1960's. She was wearing a short red polka-dot dress, her coltish legs bare and unbelievably long. Above the decal her Dad Bill had painted in black box letters "Tillie". The 'old girl' as Anna's dad had always called her, was almost 40 years old now. The essential piece of farming equipment had been lovingly taken care of year after year.

Life had a way of slowly coming back together. Daily chores and routine gave a sense of normalcy to what was once chaos and uncertainty. Anna had let her job at the library go. It had been a painful decision, yet one she felt she really had no other choice. The media onslaught had finally tapered off to a few reporters showing up now and then. There was no story if there was no access to her family. Eddie made sure that would not happen. Allyson had gotten a job in nearby Carmel, working for a clinical oncologist office as a nurse. Both Eddie and Jane returned to their daily routines and jobs as well. Still, Anna rarely ever ventured away from the farm. The house in town remain closed for now. She hoped one day that Allyson would want to have it for her own.

The dreams of the futuristic world had been coming nightly for months. They occupied her mind during the day and they were what she thought of as she carefully drove along the fields planting seed. The dreams had changed. Instead of standing on the hill talking to the gray-haired lady, Anna had been in the valley talking to the people there. She had the same strange conversations with each of them, hearing them talk to her and hearing her own voice replying, yet again, she never noticed any movements of their mouths. Anna could only surmise that these people did not speak in her language, yet somehow could understand each other perfectly. Telepathy? Anna didn't know.

Each person she talked to, the men and women, seemed just like any other person she met in her life time. Their human characteristics were just like her own. The colors of their eyes, hair and skin were familiar as well, from the palest skin to the darkest hue. Only the manner of dress was different. It consisted of pale colored robes of some material Anna could not discern.

Every person that she talked to had something to teach her about their world. They discussed the way they got energy needed to power their world from the sun and wind, turbines and greenhouses. They showed her ways crops could be grown without soil and how to turn the oceans saltwater into freshwater. Anna would routinely wake at 12:12 am and rush to write as much as she could remember into her journals, drawing clumsy pictures of all that she had seen.

As she rounded a corner of the field, Anna smiled, remembering the children that played around the town. They had looked at her curiously and waved at her, but she never talked to any of them. She remembered however, the sound of their childish laughter and sweet voices as they called to each other, playing strange games that Anna puzzled over.

The old tractor started to cough and sputter as Anna released the clutch. As she tried to change gears all she heard was a loud grinding noise. She braked to a slow stop and idled the engine, listening to the motor. Again, she tried to change gears, but the clutch remained stuck.

"Shit!" Anna said aloud. She turned off the engine and sat there a moment trying to think. She was a ways from the house and had forgotten to bring her cell phone. No one was home at the moment anyway.

"Hey! Do you need any help there?" Eric Alexander called across from the barbed wire fence. The soybean field was very close to the boundary that separated the two properties.

Anna turned and saw him waving at her. She had finally gotten used to seeing him walking on his property, or driving his small tractor, or doing daily chores. She had even waved back at him occasionally as he lifted a hand in greeting. Now, she waved dismissively back at him then jumped down from the cab and walked around the tractor, hands on her hips. Why did this have to happen her first time planting? The dang tractor had lasted 40 years.

Anna kicked the tractor tire in frustration. "Come, on Tillie! Help a woman out here!"

"Who is Tillie?"

Anna turned to look again at her neighbor, her frustration mounting. However he was nowhere to be seen.

"Excuse me?" she said as she walked around the tractor. And then finally, she spotted Eric Alexander. He was lying face down on the ground, half way between the last two wires in the barbed fence. He was stuck.

"What the hell are you doing?"

"I thought you needed help," he said sheepishly.

He propped his elbows in front of him in the new grass and looked over at Anna Anderson looking back at him with clear annoyance. Her hands were on her hips, her slim legs looked fetchingly in faded jeans. Her blue t-shirt was damp and clung to her shapely chest. As he watched her take the cap off her hair and wipe the sweat off her face, Eric thought he had never seen a sexier woman in his life.

Anna sighed and walked towards him. He was under the wire near his waistline. She glanced down his long body, encased in jeans and a brown t-shirt. Some of the barbed fence had ripped a gap in the back pocket of his pants, exposing part of his muscular thigh and dark blue underwear. Another tine was embedded in the cotton of his t-shirt.

"That fence is there for a reason, Mr. Alexander."

"To keep the animals from getting out?"

"To keep nosey neighbors from getting in," she replied as she bent down to consider how to go about getting him out of there. She tried to avert her eyes from his exposed thigh and the curved roundness of his ass.

"Where's your cell phone?" she asked him.

"In my house."

Anna glanced across the fence and the rows of sowed fields to the gray farmhouse in the distance. There was no help for it. She was going to have to get him out of there by herself. She considered for a moment just leaving him lying there like some prone scarecrow. She chuckled in amusement at the idea.

"What's so funny?" he said looking up at her smiling face. He was glad she wasn't looking at him in annoyance any longer. She was really lovely when she smiled.

"I doubt you would consider it amusing," she said then eyed his clothes again. "I'm going to have to rip your back pocket off and most of your t-shirt."

"I don't usually let women do that until the fourth date," he said, and gave her a lopsided grin.

Anna felt herself blushing. He had clear blue eyes, crinkled at the corners. He was a man who probably laughed often, she thought. His thick blondish-gray hair was cut short and she could smell a masculine herbal scent coming from it as she bent down to check his shirt. She looked away from his probing eyes and took a deep breath and tried to gather her thoughts.

She grasped the back pocket of his jeans and gave a strong pull. The fabric was tough. She gave it a few more strong tugs and finally the pocket and barb came off. So much of his buttock was now exposed that it disturbed Anna's composure to look at it. She swiftly moved to his t-shirt and ripped that away from the other barb.

"Okay, I'm going to hold the fence as high as I can. Just try and crawl through."

"Yes, Ma'am," he said and tried to squirm out from under the fence. As one of the tines drew a long scratch down the middle of his exposed thighs, he winced.

"Oh, I'm sorry!" she told him and placed the ripped pocket over the tine that had scratched him. "Try again."

By wiggling like an army recruit through a battlefield he finally got to the other side of the fence. He stood up shakily and gave her another one of those lop-sided grins.

He stuck out his right hand to shake, and said, "I'm Eric Alexander, but you must have guessed that."

Anna frowned at him for a moment then stuck out her own hand and muttered her own name.

The scratch on his thigh was bleeding a little bit. She used the piece of torn t-shirt and wiped the blood as best as she could.

Eric just stood stock still, even though it hurt like hell.

"You need to get that taken care of."

"I will. Thank you for rescuing me, m'lady," he said and with an awkward flourish he bowed. "What kind of knight in shining armor am I? You probably didn't need me at all."

A look of sadness came over her face and Eric was immediately contrite. He wasn't sure what he had said or did to cause it but the pain that crossed her face affected him as well.

"I no longer need to be saved," she said and walked back to the tractor.

Eric followed her with as much dignity as he could muster knowing that most of the right side of his back pants had ripped away and was exposing his underwear. He watched Anna climb in the cab and start the engine again. She tried to shift it into gear but it wouldn't budge.

"I'm no mechanic but I'm pretty sure it's a broken clutch," she muttered. She got down off the seat and motioned for him to give it a try.

Eric climbed into the tractor can and tried shifting the gears. He could hear them grinding.

"Yeah, that's the clutch alright. You might have burnt a disc. I suggest you get the transmission looked at and get the bearings and flywheel checked," he said as he turned the engine off and climbed down.

Anna groaned with frustration. She wasn't even a quarter done with planting this field. It would mean a delay.

"I'll call Robbie Miller and have him come take a look at it in the morning." she said.

"Robbie Miller, our neighbor?"

"Yes. The only neighbor I usually allow on my property," she said and lifted her eyebrow. "Well, you can't go home the way you came in. Come on back to the house and I'll drive you home."

"I don't want to be any trouble."

"It's kind of late for that isn't it?" she said and watched the smile come off his handsome face. "I'm only joking, Mr. Alexander."

"Eric. I think a woman who has seen my buttocks should use my first name," he replied. The smile curved up and widened, showing straight white teeth.

Anna started the long walk to the house. Eric caught up to her and matched her strides with his own.

"My mother used to tell me to always wear clean underwear and never play poker with millionaires. I'm glad I've taken her advice so far," he said again.

Anna came to a stop and looked up at him, shielding her eyes from the mid-day sun. He really was tall.

"I sense that you are trying to be funny," she said.

"It keeps me from running away in embarrassment."

Finally, Anna's mouth lifted at the corners in a smile. For some unknown reason, she was actually feeling very comfortable in his presence.

For the rest of the walk, they talked about farming and planting. She made a few suggestions to him about farming techniques that surprised him. He wondered how she seemed to know so much about agriculture, but her family had been farmers a very long time. He supposed that it just came naturally to her.

"Come on in. I'll take care of that scratch for you," she said as they walked up the porch of the white farmhouse and entered the front door.

Once inside the cool interior of the house, Anna pointed to a chair, told him to make himself comfortable, and left him there. The house wasn't big or modern but it was very homey and uncluttered. The furniture was worn and out-dated but everything was very clean. An old upright piano stood against a wall in the living area.

Anna returned carrying a first-aid kit. She was all non-nonsense as she asked him to turn around and bare his backside to her. She bent down and eyed his injured skin.

He felt her gentle hands as she cleaned the scratch with antiseptic. He winced at the sting of the spray but didn't move. Mostly he concentrated on her hands.

"You know, I'm sorry you got hurt but it really was funny," she said as she spread ointment on the injury.

Eric heard her snort, then chuckle, Soon, she was laughing out loud and he followed suit.

The two of them laughed so hard they never noticed Eddie and Jane standing in the doorway looking at them in surprise.

Anna's face was right next to their neighbor's ass. Her hand was on the back of his thigh. They were both laughing uncontrollably. "What's going on here?" Eddie said.

Anna tried to stand up but fell on her butt. Eric bent down to help her, and unbeknownst to him, gave Eddie and Jane a good look at his ripped pants, underwear and naked thigh.

"Well, hello!" Jane said eyeing the rip. She held out her hand to shake. "I'm Jane Monroe. It's nice to meet you."

Eric took Jane's hand and shook it.

"It's nice to meet you, Mrs. Monroe."

"Oh, I think you can call me Jane now," she told him with an amused look.

Eddie rolled his eyes at his wife. Then he looked from Anna to Eric and back again. What was going on? This was definitely interesting, indeed.

"Now that we've seen your ass, I think you should stay for dinner," Eddie said.

***

Later that night, Eddie sat in the comfortable old chair in his den and thought about his sister and Eric Alexander. Anna had acted flustered every time she'd looked at her neighbor. Allyson and Mark had joined the four of them for pizza and they'd all chatted around the old kitchen table as they ate dinner. Later on Anna played the piano for them and they had sang songs and told tales from their family histories. It had been fun and relaxing. Most of all Eddie, Jane, and Allyson were all so happy to see Anna smiling and full of life.

The last few months had been so difficult for all of them, especially for her. There were times that her sense of joviality seemed forced and strained. Anna had moments of sadness and melancholy from missing Andy and there was a part of her that seemed unreachable.

Eddie had worried that the farm had become a jail cell for her but she assured him over and over that she was content with things as they were. One day the attention over her disappearance would die and she would begin to feel comfortable venturing out again and letting more people into her life. People like Eric Alexander.

Eddie had finally stopped asking her if she remembered anything at all about those missing nine days. The police officer in him wanted to keep digging for details and answers and to look for some kind of closure. He also sensed that Anna might actually have some idea about what had really happened. He didn't know if she was struggling with it or that the answers were so incredible that she could not comprehend the truth.

Eddie himself wondered if it was better to never know about what really happened. Both Jane and Allyson kept telling him to just be grateful for the wonderful gift of Anna's return and to let it go.

One day, his sister might tell him the truth about what she believed had happened to her, but if, and until then he would be content to be thankful for everything they had all been given.

CHAPTER TWENTY FIVE

Anna sat on the old couch watching Eric Alexander as he sat opposite in the heavy, over-stuffed chair in the living room of her farmhouse, sipping from a glass of red wine. They had a quiet dinner earlier, making small talk about both their farms. They also talked briefly about her family's history and he discussed his new classes and students at college.

Summer had ended and school had started more than a month before. Soon both farms would be harvesting their last crops. It had been a very busy summer and Anna was thrilled the way her fist real season as a full time farmer had gone. There had been plenty of glitches but she had learned so much from each mistake and from the knowledge she obtained through hard work and educating herself.

It had all happened because of her dreams. The things she'd learned about farming and plants and solar power turned out to be very helpful to her daily work life. She'd also shared this knowledge with Eric. He was astounded at the techniques she'd suggested to him. When he'd asked where she had learned such things. Anna remained evasive, telling him that she learned them from online search.

There was something about Eric that had made Anna trust him almost immediately. It helped that their first meeting had been full of hilarity. Even now, Anna would think about that day and smile.

Eric never asked her questions about her disappearance or tried to probe into her private life. She had come to believe that she could share her deepest feelings with him.

He was obviously attracted to her, but she did not know how to handle that emotion from him. What confused her even more was were her own budding but tentative feelings of happiness about their friendship. It was becoming a comfortable and rewarding relationship, but she wasn't sure she wanted it to become more than that.

Maybe it was the three glasses of wine Anna had consumed or perhaps it was just the need to finally tell someone. Whatever the reason, she felt a compelling need to reveal the truth about what she believed really happened to her, to this man. She started to tell the story like it was one of her own tall tales.

"Once upon a time, there was this woman named Anna. On her 50th birthday, at an exact time on a certain day, this car was hit broadside on the passenger side where Anna was sitting. When witnesses to the accident came upon this car, they should have found Anna in the passenger seat, but she was gone. She just...disappeared."

"Where did she go?" Eric asked.

"She went to another place and another time. A place different from her world, yet there were similarities in the people in this futuristic place to her own. The children laughed and played like any other children Anna knew. They spoke in a different language but somehow she still understood them in her own. They lived in a beautiful valley with snow capped mountains and a large body of water in the distance. There were solar homes and solar technology all around the town. There were wind turbines running up and down the hills like giant metal spinning crosses. It was a place of peace...and hope."

Eric carefully put his glass of wine on the coffee table, never taking his eyes off of Anna. He was trying to keep his face blank but inside he felt a furious onslaught of emotion. Was she telling him a story or the truth about what happened to her?

"Anna went to this place in the future that had the medical technology to change so many things about her, including her hearing. When she came back to Earth almost a week and a half later, it was almost like she was a different person."

"How did she get there Anna? How did she go from the middle of a car accident to another...place and time?"

"Anna was hoping that perhaps you could tell her."

Eric looked at her in astonishment, "Why do you think I know how to do that?" he said. Was she nuts? He glanced at her earnest face and remembered the conversations he'd had with her all spring and summer. She always struck him as honest and straight-forward. No, she wasn't crazy.

Anna got up from the couch a bit unsteadily and walked through the short hallway to her bedroom. She opened the top drawer to her writing desk and took out a folder and carried it back to the living room. She took out copies of the photos of the accident and the police reports and laid the pictures on the coffee table in front of Eric.

"See this picture of the bank marquee across the street from the accident? 12:12 pm," she said as she shuffled through each picture. "Do you see this picture that was taken by a witness to the accident as it happened? There is this tiny white flash on the passenger side even though it was raining that day. There is a connection there. I think you could help me comprehend what it all is."

Eric picked up each picture and studied them thoroughly. He was amazed at the pictures of Jane Monroe's demolished car. The passenger side no longer even existed. But, she hadn't been there, had she? She was trying to tell him she disappeared at that moment of impact.

Eric rubbed his hands across his face. He was a man of science. He was interested in the examination and studious inquiry of accumulated data to form intelligent conclusions. Nothing about what happened to Anna was logical, but she was asking him to explain it to her.

"Okay, let me think. The accident happened on 12-12-2012 at 12:12 pm. The connection is in the timing somehow," he said.

"I know that much, Eric," she told him and frowned. "I want to know how."

"I'd have to take a wild guess, Anna. That is not going to make it plausible or even realistic."

"I still want you to try and explain it," she looked at him imploringly.

He could see it on her face that she trusted him and that realization pleased him immensely. At that moment he wanted nothing more than to help her understand what had happened to her. He looked down at the pictures again, studying each one closely. He thought about the 'story' she just told him about this futuristic world and didn't doubt any longer that she truly believed she had gone to this place.

"OK. Somehow, on 12-12-2012 at 12:12 pm a portal through time opened up at the impact of the accident and you went through it," he said to her, pointing at the picture with the white flash. Even as he heard himself say it, he knew how ridiculous it sounded.

"A portal through time," she repeated.

"You went to this place and that was how you...changed." he continued, guessing.

Anna sat there thinking about what he was saying. It all seemed absurd and illogical and even improbable. She knew he was only guessing, but somehow, his words were incredibly exciting. She wasn't crazy!

"I keep having dreams of this futuristic place and seeing all those things I described. So far it all seemed to have happened in just one day. I always see the sky as blue and the sun shining. It never gets dark," she said and went on to describe the town and people to him.

Eric listened with rapt attention to each revelation. She told him about the conversations she had had with this older woman and the people who lived in the quaint town and about Earth's apocalyptic future. Although it did not take a huge stretch of the imagination to believe such a thing could happen, listening to her tell it was almost like reading a good science fiction story.

"I returned on the highway outside of town on 12-21-2012 at 12:12 am. I don't know how I got there either. What do you think that means, Eric?" she asked him again.

"12-21-2012," he said and leaned back in his chair. "Do you knows what that date signifies, Anna?"

"It was supposed to be the end of the world, according to the Mayan calendar," she said with a smile.

"Right. It was revealed and later disputed that the Mayans believed a range of cataclysmic events would occur on or around December 21st, 2012 and end life on Earth as we know it. What the Mayans actually believed was that this date was the end of one cycle and beginning of another. However, that is nothing new. December 21st is the beginning of winter solstice. It's a time of change."

"I was gone nine days. I still don't understand how or why."

"Nine days of Earth time, Anna," he said. "Perhaps it was only a moment in time through space."

"That makes sense, but it doesn't explain how I got back. I also don't know why me. I'm sure in all the world on that day and time there must have been other people who were in an accident at that exact moment. Why did this happen to me?"

Eric shook his head. He had no guess for that.

"Are you still having these dreams?" he asked her.

"Yes."

"Perhaps one day you will know why."

"None of this sounds possible does it?" she asked. "I tell myself it's all preposterous, yet here I am. Something did happen or I wouldn't be sitting here."

"Truth is singular, Anna. People believe what they want to believe despite the logistics of a perceived truth. Sometimes this truth is an illusion of reality."

"You don't believe me then, do you?"

Eric searched her face. The scientist in him was still skeptical, yet what conclusion could he draw from what happened to her? Anna knew things about farming that she had no formal training or education for, methods he'd never heard of anyone using. Where could she have gotten this knowledge?

"I've lived my life so long with the need to have scientific study to draw coherent conclusions from data obtained from exhaustive research and detailed analysis. Yet, I've walked my fields at night and looked at the stars and felt the vastness that is our universe. I know there is so much that mankind does not know about his world and will never know. There are great mysteries with no answers. I think you are trying to untangle your own mystery and perhaps the answer to it is not logical to us, but somewhere and some place it does makes sense. Yes, Anna, I believe you."

Anna felt as though a great weight was lifted off her shoulders. She was no longer alone with this emotionally exhausting secret!

The two of them sat there in the comforting silence thinking about the things they had discussed. Once in awhile their eyes would meet and Anna would give Eric a soft smile that made his insides melt. It gave him hope that perhaps someday they could explore this undeniable connection and chemistry that existed between them.

"What if I am a clone, Eric?" she asked him suddenly.

Anna had come upon a bunch of tabloids in the trash out back waiting to be burned. She suspected that Allyson had been trying to keep her from seeing them. At first she laughed as she read some of the stories, but some of them left her with disquiet misgiving.

"What? You can't be serious?" Eric laughed, but he saw the solemn look on her face and leaned forward in his chair.

"Anna, you are not a clone because there is no reason for them to do that, right? This woman told you they have the best medical technology there ever could be. You are proof of what they could do. Why make a clone of you at all when all they needed to do was tweak a few things? You were already pretty darn perfect, if you ask me."

A tentative smile emerged on her face.

"Well, if they would have asked me I would have told them to make me taller. I'd have liked a smaller ass too. However, the perky breasts are great!" she said, and laughed out loud.

"Wh...what?" Eric said. It was suddenly taking all his concentration to keep looking at her face.

He felt himself blushing and covered his eyes with his hands. He heard her laughing and it was sweet music to his ears. He looked at her through his fingers and smiled at her amusement and wanted to kiss her so badly, but again, there was this thing called timing. He would be her friend and hope for more one day when the timing was right.

***

They stood on the hill again, overlooking the tranquil valley. Anna let the sense of peace she always felt when she stood there wash over her in soothing waves.

"I don't think I ever asked your name," she said to the gray-haired lady.

The woman smiled back at her gently. "I was named after my grandmother and her grandmother before her. There is a long line of women in my family with this name."

"What is it?" she asked her.

"Anna, just like yours, my dear."

Anna? This woman had the same name as her! Anna looked at her in astonishment.

"One of the very first women who arrived here almost a thousand years ago was named Anna as well. She was a great scientist and innovator. She was part of this shuttle of others who had dreams of a new world. Every other daughter in her family that came after her was also given this name in her honor," she paused. *"This woman is your descendant, Anna. You are part of our family history. We are your future."*

Anna stared with amazement into the woman's eyes. Blue eyes, that looked like her Mother Maria's, and just like her own. "Why did you tell me about the destruction and desolation of my world? There isn't really anything I can do about this, is there?"

"You can take from this world what you have learned from the people here. You can teach this to others Anna, but no, you can't really stop any of that from happening on Earth. You can pass this knowledge on down to the next generations in your family but you can't change the actions of others. That path to total destruction started way before your time," she told Anna sadly. *"It's too late. I didn't tell you about the future to prevent it from happening, but so that life in this new world would prosper. The only thing you can do now is ensure that our family survives."*

"Even now, this place you see here in this beautiful valley is perceived as ancient and out-dated by others. There are bigger, more modern cities on the other side of the mountains and waters. I still have hope that we won't repeat the same mistakes from the past."

She reached up to touch the pendant she wore around her neck. She caressed the blue stone with her forefinger and it emitted a soft light. And then she took the pendant from around her neck and handed to her ancestor.

"We call this pendant 'rerum tanta novitas', which means 'rebirth' in your language. It has been passed down from generation to generation. Your being here started a wave of events that changed our course. One day you are going to need this to assure that future continues. You will know when that time comes. It will only happen once Anna, so trust in yourself."

Anna took the pendant from her carefully. She could feel its warmth and power.

"How will I know when it's time?"

"Trust yourself, Anna. You will know."

Anna awoke with a start, not bothering to glance at the clock. It was always the same. What had the Anna from the future meant when she said "Your being here started a wave of events that changed our course"? Was she talking about Anna's accident? Did that mean it was never supposed to happen?

As she lay in her bed at the farmhouse, in the room where her parents had slept for so many years, her mind traveled back to the early morning hours of December 21st, 2012 as she stood in her bathroom looking in the mirror.

Anna had stood there holding her toothbrush, wondering who this woman was staring back at her in the mirror was. As her daughter slept in the next room beyond the closed bathroom door, Anna had set down heavily on the wooden bathroom bench clutching the warm towel around herself.

She'd leaned down and picked up her dark blue cable-knit sweater off the floor where she'd laid it, and run her hands over it as searching for clues to where she may have been. The soft threads revealed nothing. Anna picked up her black slacks and looked them over as well. She reached into her right pocket and felt something hard. Her hand grasped the object and slowly pulled it out of the pocket.

In her hands was a very strange looking pendant. There was intricately laced metal of some kind in a diamond shape, surrounding a light blue stone in the middle. The metal was neither silver or bronze, but something she was unsure of. Anna had run her hands around and over the pendant. She thought the blue stone flashed for a second but it could have been just the light. On the side was a tiny metal clasp. She gently touched it and the blue stone came open to show a tiny object in a soft bed underneath. The miniscule object looked like half the size of a blue cold capsule. Looking at it gave her a jolt of trepidation. Where had it come from? What was she doing with it in her pocket?

Although the pendant gave off a feeling of warmth, Anna was afraid. There was something about this piece of jewelry and the tiny blue capsule that also emitted a sense of power that she didn't understand. Until she did, she would keep the find of it to herself. She closed the stone quickly and reaching into her vanity drawer she retrieved one of her mother Maria's soft white handkerchiefs and wrapped the pendant carefully inside it. She had gotten up and opened the bathroom closet and placed the wrapped handkerchief in an old jewelry box at the back.

Now, months later, Anna finally understood what that power the pendant entailed. One day she would need to use it to ensure her families future. How that would happen and when, she did not know. She opened up the bedside table drawer and reached inside. Beneath one of her journals was the pendant wrapped in her mother's handkerchief. Anna took the pendant out carefully and held it in the palm of her hand. She had looked at it almost every single day since that first night, not truly understanding its meaning, but now she did. She would wear it every single day from this day forward.

One great cycle ended and another had begun. That's what Eric had said about the date 12-21-2012. She looked down at the pendant in her hand and whispered "rerum tanta novitas". The rebirth of a new life.

CHAPTER TWENTY SIX

Allyson stood watching her mother as she blew out the single candle on her birthday cake. She looked so lovely wearing a soft baby blue sweater and blue jeans. Her blonde hair was pulled into a simple ponytail. Allyson shook her head and laughed quietly to herself. Her mother looked so young! They could have been sisters.

The small cake decorated in shades of pink, the lettering stating simply *"Happy Birthday Anna! 50+1"*. Allyson closed her eyes and gave a quick prayer of thanks for everything that had happened this past year. Thanks that her mother was standing there in front of her, thanks that their relationship had been repaired and they were closer than they'd ever been. She was thankful for the long talks they had about life and being about to share with her the wonderful moments of falling in love with Mark and hopes and dreams for their future.

Earlier that afternoon, her Uncle Eddie and Aunt Jane had come by to spend the day with them. As 12:12 pm approached the three of them had gotten more and more uneasy. Their small talk was stilted with long uncomfortable pauses as each of them watched Anna almost constantly. They stood around her in a protective circle around the kitchen island, preparing food for the party, trying not to be obvious.

"OK, back away before one of you gets tasered with cheese spread," Anna said jokingly as she held out a canister of processed cheese spread and aimed it at the three of them.

"I think that's a felony, lady." Eddie said, doing his best to sound serious, but after a moment he gave a wry chuckle. He glanced down at his watch. It was almost time.

"Seriously, what do you think might happen?" Anna asked.

"Nothing!" they all said at once, looking back and forth at each other uneasily. The clock on the microwave hit 12:12 and they held their breath watching Anna. She shook her head at them, but her looked turned sympathetic as she saw their obvious distress. Allyson was close to tears, clasping her hands tightly together, her knuckles showing white. Eddie was clenching his jaw, running his hands through his hair, a sure sign that he was nervous. Jane's lovely face was so pale in contrast with her red silk blouse, her eyes blinking open and closed in agitation.

Finally the minute passed and the three of them gave a loud gasp of relief.

"I need a drink!" Eddie said and headed to the refrigerator.

"Give me one!" Allyson said, reaching past her uncle's arm and grabbing a bottle of beer.

"I think something stronger is called for," Jane said from the dining room and walked into the kitchen holding a bottle of whiskey and four shot glasses. "Let's get this party started!"

Now, Allyson watched her mother cutting the cake. They'd eaten a small birthday lunch and drank heartily. After the tense moments with the clock, they'd been able to relax and enjoy themselves. Just a moment ago, the three of them had sung "Happy Birthday" to Anna. She'd closed her eyes and listened to them with a smile on her face. There were tears in her eyes when they finished the song with gusto. Anna had laughed and thanked them, hugging and kissing each of them.

They'd sat outside on the patio, enjoying their cake, sitting in chairs around a small brick fire pit that Grandpa Monroe had built years ago. They wore jackets and hats but it was 50 degrees and the sun was shining brightly. Both the sun and the fire gave off a pleasant warmth. Later that night they'd have a larger dinner with both Mark and Eric invited. For now they enjoyed their intimate time as a family.

"I have a story," Anna said all of a sudden. She'd finished her cake and put the plate down on a side table.

Allyson was surprised by this announcement. She hadn't hear her mother tell a story in such a long time.

"There was a young fox that lived in the forest alone. Every day he'd wake up at a certain time, eat his breakfast and do his household chores always the same way. He would take his daily walk through the deep woods and get home at the same time. He would have his dinner and go to bed. Everything was a constant circle of predictable repetition," Anna said.

Allyson listened to her mother with puzzlement. This was unlike any other story she'd told. Most of her stories were silly and comical, whichever made the listener laugh the most.

Anna continued her story.

"One day as the fox walked through the forest counting his steps so that he'd make it home at his usual time, a newborn baby bird fell out of a tree as the fox walked beneath it. The baby bird landed on the ground at his feet, interrupting him. The fox looked in anxious agitation at this sudden change in his routine. The baby bird looked up at him and gave a small "chirp". The fox looked around, unsure what to do. If he helped this bird, his whole day would be ruined! He stood there quivering in indecision. He could continue on, walking a bit faster and soon he'd make the time up. But, as he looked down at the helpless little bird, he knew it was too late. If he left the bird on the ground it would fall prey to the other forest animals. How could he let that happen? Sighing, the fox gently picked up the baby bird and scurried up the tree, holding the bird securely with his tail. He placed him carefully back in the nest and patted him on the head with a smile. Every day after that, the bird visited the fox. Messing up his house and getting food on the floor, yet the fox was happy for the first time in his life. The fox ran through the forest now as the little bird flew above him. He was no longer conscious of time. He had a friend!" she said.

There was a long pause as Allyson, Eddie and Jane looked at Anna. The story perplexed them.

"I suppose there's a moral to this story?" Eddie asked Anna finally.

"Being in the right place at the right time, can change your whole life. It can be considered a kind of miracle," Anna said. Then she got up from her chair and turned to look at her brother for a long moment. "Just as being in the wrong place at the wrong time can also change a life and the lives of all those that surround that person. It won't be a miracle, but a tragedy."

Allyson watched as her mother continued to stare at her uncle. There was something tangible passing between them. An understanding? Whatever it was, she noticed the change in her Uncle Eddie. There was an unmistakable sadness in his face as if he'd come to the realization about something. Whatever it was, it made Allyson afraid.

***

The two of them sat in Eric's truck in the First Presbyterian Church parking lot. It was after midnight the morning on December 21st. Other than Eric's black truck, the parking lot was empty.

Anna had asked Eric to drive her to the spot where she had reappeared a year earlier. They'd parked his truck at the church and walked down the hill. She stood at the spot she thought she had come to awareness of her surroundings on that cold night a year ago. She looked up at the sky. It all looked so familiar. Clear and black, the stars twinkling overhead like jewels on black velvet, her breath creating a misty fog, surrounding her head like a smoky Christmas wreath. She remembered the feeling of panic and fear that had racked her body as she had stood there, wondering what had happened to her. Now, she felt a sense of calmness and relief.

Eric stood on the side of the highway with his hands in his

173

pockets, watching her in the middle of the road.

Anna kept looking up at the sky. How had she gotten back here? No matter how many times she questioned it, there was no logical explanation. She'd come back here in the same way she'd left, an unanswered mystery. 'A portal through time' Eric had said. Anna chuckled out loud at how absurd it still sounded, even in her head.

"What's so funny?" Eric asked, moving toward her.

"Everything," she said, watching him as he came to stand beside her. "Life."

It made her think of Andy and how he'd seemed to find amusement at even the darkest times in his life. He would have found the whole story about Anna's life this past year hilarious. "Find a way to enjoy life's funny moments again" he'd said to her. Now she understood what he meant. She took a deep breath of the clean, cold night air and felt the tear in her heart begin to mend.

Eric smiled down at her and brushed her soft hair away from her face.

"One morning I got up at 6 am and wondered "where did the sun go?" and then it dawned on me,..." he said and smiled at her as she shook her head at him and gave an un-lady like snort. "I saw you standing on your side of the fence next to a broken down tractor, listening to you curse at it...and the sun never stopped shining for me since that day."

Anna looked up at him, listening to his voice change from one of amusement to something else altogether.

She stood on her toes and reached up and kissed him fully on the mouth. It was a wonderful deep passionate kiss, full of yearning and potential. When the kiss ended, they both laughed out loud and hugged each other close. Anna glanced over Eric's shoulder at the church marquee in the background. Sure enough it said 12:12. Timing and second chances she thought to herself. That's what this was all about.

***

Inside the truck Anna took out the pendant from underneath her coat and sweater and pulled it over her head, handing it to Eric. He took it from her gently with a quizzical look on his face.

"What is it?" he asked her.

"Proof."

Eric shook his head at her, not understanding.

"It was given to me by the gray-haired lady from the future. She wore it around her neck. She told me that one day I would need to use it."

Anna leaned forward and touched the clasp on the side of the pendant and pulled up the blue stone to reveal the tiny blue capsule beneath.

Eric touched the capsule in astonishment. Surely this was indeed proof of the stories she'd told him about in her dreams! This jewelry was unlike anything he'd ever seen.

"Through my dreams and what I've learned and all the reading and research about this capsule design, the closest thing I can come up with is it is some kind of nanotechnology. I think this is the same kind of technology that 'changed' me."

Eric knew what nanotechnology was. It was the manipulation of atomic matter on an incredible tiny scale. Although he considered himself a scientist, nanotechnology definitely wasn't his field of expertise.

"I've had this since I reappeared on the night of December 21st. One year ago."

"What is it for, Anna?"

"To ensure the future."

CHAPTER TWENTY SEVEN
DECEMBER 12, 2021

On the morning of Anna's 59th birthday, she lay in bed trying to ease the anxiety that this date always brought about. Nine years. It all had gone by so quickly! So much of it had seemed like a blur. Eddie and Jane still came to see her every few days. Anna had stopped protesting their need to keep an eye on her, even after all this time. Eddie was still the Chief of police in Greenway but he was getting ready to retire in the next year, or so he said. Anna smiled to herself thinking that while her brother had grand ideas about traveling and fishing and sitting on the porch and drinking beer, she had a difficult time imaging him ever being idle. Anna had offered him and Jane the farmhouse, but Eddie said he was content just to come out in the Spring and Fall and drive the tractor around for a few hours.

Eric helped her install the solar panels on the farmhouse roof after she had it replaced a few years ago. There were two wind turbines in the fields and even a windmill and a greenhouse close to the barn out back. In 2015, the farm's growing methods had become organic. It had taken much work and effort to make it all productive. Farming really was back-breaking labor but Anna always felt such a sense of accomplishment as she looked out onto the growing corn or soybeans and hay that grew each season. She lovingly tended to her own vegetable garden and learned to can and freeze for the winter months.

She had fallen in love with Eric along the way, but it had been such a different love from the kind she'd had with Andy. The nine years had helped eased the pain of his passing, yet she still thought of him every single day. She carried the memory of her time with Andy on herself like an ever-present shadow.

Eric was such a good, kind and sweet man. He was so generous with his time, helping her with the farm and teaching her everything he knew about agriculture and solar energy. They lived separately, he on his own farm next door, she on hers, but they saw each other almost every day. He still taught at the community college, and both he and Anna had set aside acreage on their farms just for his students.

Eric had asked Anna twice to marry him. Each time she had gently told him she wasn't ready. He'd taken the answer calmly and patiently. She felt they both knew and understood that one day her answer would be different.

Every year on the anniversary of her disappearance, the media ascended on the small farming community seeking answers, but most of these were now just tabloid reporters. When people don't have the answers they seek, they tend to make them up on their own. Most had decided Anna's story was some elaborate hoax. Anna had never consented to another interview and there were too many questions about her disappearance and few answers. The people of the rural town had also closed ranks around her and her family in a tight-knit circle of protection, and refused to discuss the event with reporters.

Even so, Anna rarely ventured further than town. Once in awhile she took a trip into Indianapolis or Chicago, hoping no one recognized her. She never went back to work at the library and augmented her income with farming.

The farm could have felt like a prison with the almost constant need to surround herself in its warm folds, but instead she turned it into her own sanctuary. The soil of this farm had imprinted a lasting impression on her skin, it had become ingrained in her soul.

The biggest change in the last nine years had been the marriage of

Allyson and Mark seven years before. Anna remembered the incredible pride and happiness she had felt as she stood at the altar wearing her light purple matron-of-honor gown in the small church and watched her brother Eddie walk his niece up the aisle. Allyson had worn the very same wedding dress she had worn to marry Andy, and her antique veil had been the same worn by both Anna and her grandmother Maria at their own weddings. It had been a wonderful day.

Allyson had taken a job at a university hospital in Indianapolis and Mark still worked for the Greenway police department with Eddie. They had bought the home Allyson had grown up in and Anna was overjoyed that the house would stay in the family and be part of so many more happy memories.

Best of all there was their child. Tiny, dark-haired Annabelle had been born four years ago and Anna had fallen in love with her granddaughter immediately. She had been in the delivery room when this precious bundle took her first breath. Annabelle had not cried at all after being born, but merely laid in her mother's arms and looked at the world questioningly through tiny squinted eyes.

Anna had gotten what Allyson called "over-bearing grandmother-itis". She purchased so many clothes and toys and stuffed animals that Mark joked that they needed the spare bedroom just to house little Annabelle's own private "zoo". The farmhouse was filled with photo after photo of events from her granddaughter's life.

"I don't think you have enough pictures, Mom," Allyson said one day as she stood in the living room of the farmhouse and looked around at frame after frame of pictures of Annabelle.

"What? Are you serious? What did I miss?" Anna asked her daughter.

"It's a joke, Mom! This child has been photographed more times than any Royal baby in the history of Royal babies."

Fortunately, Annabelle acted nothing like a princess. She fussed at any attempts to put her in frilly dresses and cute little shoes with bows, and was happiest in just her diaper or nothing at all. A worn out Allyson and Mark had given up their daily chase of their tiny toddler who loved to ditch her clothes and streak through the house every chance she got. For that very reason she had been potty-trained at an early age fairly easily. She now wore jeans and t-shirts and her red tennis shoes or boots most of the time. She also got dirty often around the farm, but Anna let her be a kid. A farm was a good place to run and play and smear mud around your clothing at. At least she always returned the little one back to her parents clean and fresh smelling, she thought with a chuckle.

As Anna thought about her dark-haired bundle of pure joy, her heart lifted. Annabelle bore a striking resemblance to her grandfather. She'd compared her pictures to the baby pictures she had of Andy, and the similarities were striking. They both had dark hair and chubby round cheeks, and even the shape of their noses and eyes were the same. The only difference was the eye color. Annabelle's eyes were just like her grandmother's, Monroe blue.

Eddie and Jane also doted on their grand-niece just like if she had been their own granddaughter. They took Annabelle to zoos and parks and aquariums, all the places that Anna was not yet comfortable venturing to. But she would, one day. She knew she'd need to do more things now that she had this grandchild to help educate and grow. She would need to step out of her comfort zone.

Anna got up and reached for her clothes. When she caught her reflection in the mirror over her dresser she gave her disheveled self a half-hearted grin. She had changed little in the last nine years. Sure, there were more lines around her face, and her hair, cut to her shoulder now, had more gray. Still, she thought she looked pretty good for an 'old' lady approaching sixty.

Before she went downstairs, she pulled open the drawer on her bedside table and pulled out the pendant. She'd worn it around her neck every day for the last eight years, tucked under her clothing. The dreams had stopped coming when she began putting it on, finally revealing to her the power of this pendant.

Its metal felt warm as she traced the design with her forefinger.

The light blue center seemed to come to life as she ran her finger across it, emitting a soft glow for just a second.

She had only opened the pendant twice in the time she'd had it. The night of her return and the night she'd shown it to Eric a few years ago on the first anniversary of her reappearance.

Anna had never told anyone else about it, not even her family. Now as she held the pendant again, did she wonder if she should have. Perhaps showing proof of this to her immediate family would ease their doubts and questions about those missing nine days and where she had been. Anna had used the journals she had received from Allyson that Christmas in 2012 to write down all the dreams she had about that distant place. One day she would give them to her family to read. Even now, it was hard to say they were not dreams but real memories.

In 2019 a television program aired that featured scientists discussing the discovery of a new planet just outside the Milky Way that they considered promising for habitable existence. As Anna had listened, she had known somehow that this planet the scientist had named "Spero", which was Latin for "Hope", was the place she had dreamed about. The place in her memories where she stood on the hill overlooking the town.

While it had been great news in the world of science, Anna had also watched with the realization that in order for life to exist on this new planet it would mean the ultimate destruction of their own. She had no idea how long until it would all take place. Would it be in her own lifetime, or her granddaughter's? Probably not, but happen it would. This knowledge gnawed at her soul.

***

Anna laughed as she chased Annabelle through the corn fields outside on her farm. What a gift it was to hear this sweet child's laughter! She never got tired of it.

Allyson, Mark and little Belle had come over for breakfast,

bringing doughnuts and cupcakes that Annabelle 'helped' make with her mother. Anna tried not to laugh as she viewed the lopsided and half frosted cupcakes and the one that had an obvious bite taken out of it.

Eric had come over earlier that morning, bringing her a bouquet of two dozen roses in various colors. He'd kissed her soundly, told her "Happy Birthday beautiful!" and set out to cook a breakfast casserole as they waited for the Browning's to arrive.

The five of them celebrated Anna's birthday with breakfast and toast of mimosas and plain orange juice for Annabelle. She had insisted on her own grown up flute glass and when it was her turn to make a toast she had said simply "Happy Bird-day Anna-gram!"

As they played hide and seek in the corn fields. Anna pretended not to see her granddaughter as she lay on the ground, with her little butt stuck in the air and her tiny hands around her eyes. Belle thought that if she herself couldn't see her grandmother then Anna couldn't see her either.

Allyson and Mark had gone Christmas shopping for the afternoon in Indianapolis. They would be back in time for the birthday dinner that Eddie and Jane were hosting at the farm.

Eric was standing on a ladder putting up Christmas lights along the top of the house awning and grumbling good-naturedly. He tried hard not to curse as he got his shirt sleeve caught in a nail or hit his thumbs, but he was yelling "Shoot! Shoot! Shoot!" every five minutes or so. Belle had glanced at him, her small faced scrunched up in puzzlement.

"Don't shoot the pretty lights, Eric!" she called.

"Not yet," he had told her with a chuckle, and winked at Anna. It was so warm outside. It must have been close to 70 degrees and it was only noon. Neither Anna nor Eric wore a jacket, just long sleeved t-shirts and jeans. Belle had on a long sleeved red shirt and her tiny black jeans tucked into her blue mud boots.

The weather in the Mid-west and the entire nation had been undergoing changes in the past years. It seemed like each season started later and later. The previous winter, no snow had come at all until late February. The last few summers, hurricanes had swirled in the Atlantic ocean until late November.

There had been a thunderstorm watch and warning for potential severe weather, just the night before. It certainly was crazy weather for mid-December. Anna hadn't watched the news that morning so she so she hadn't heard the day's weather forecast. The sky was overcast and tinged slightly yellow. The wind was strong, churning up puffs of dirt and dead grass. The wind chime hanging from the red barn door beat its tinkling rhythm furiously as it was battered by the sweeping air.

Belle had pleaded to come outside and play and Anna had given in, but just, she told her, until lunchtime. Though the weather seemed non-threatening earlier, now it was overcast and the wind had picked up.

"What is Sparky doing right now Anna-gram?" Belle asked her as she walked alongside her grandmother, holding tightly to her hand, through the fields after another game of hide-and-seek. Anna had waited over 10 minutes until Belle finally stopped covering her eyes so she could 'find' her. This child was tenuous indeed, Anna thought and smiled to herself. When it was Anna's turn to hide, Belle had slowly counted to ten, using some of the sign language gestures she had been taught since she was a toddler. Anna had watched her with pride from the corner of the greenhouse where she had hid.

Sparky was the name that Belle had given to the baby male Cardinal Anna had started writing a series of children's books about. The little bird lived with his parents Joseph and Mary on a farm. He bemoaned his brown feathers and yearned to be bright red like his proud Daddy. Sparky had a series of adventures on the farm and only after he learned something new from each tale would one of his brown feathers turn red. Allyson was helping Anna to illustrate each book, taking care to draw the bird family in wonderful vivid detail.

When Anna asked Belle to name each one of the birds, she stated in her little girl voice that they would be "Joseph, Mary and Sparky" forever.

Eric had whispered in Anna's ear "Joseph, Mary and *Sparky*? Isn't there supposed to be a baby Jesus in this story somewhere?" Trying not to laugh, Anna had shushed him.

"Today Sparky learns that it is okay to get wet and take a bath from two other older birds. What should we name them?"

"Phineas and Ferb."

"I think those names are already taken."

"Mickey and Minnie?"

"Nope."

Belle shrugged her shoulders and tilted her small head. "Are the new birds olden like you and Eric?"

"Yes," Anna said and bit her lip to keep from laughing.

"Pop and Nanny!"

"Okay, that's good. Pop and Nanny it is!" she told her. Belle clapped her tiny hands in glee and ran ahead through the fields towards the barn.

And then, from out of nowhere, a blast of rain began to fall, hitting the earth in a furious drumming. Anna looked up at the sky in surprise and saw a wedge of dark ominous clouds moving quickly in the distance. Then the hail started. The marble sized ice hit the ground in frantic bursts, bouncing rapidly off the surface as soon as they hit. She felt the cold wind rush over her and she started to shiver.

"Anna! Run, Anna!" Eric yelled as he tried to get down from the ladder, the wind tearing at him. He was pointing to something to the south of the farmhouse. Anna felt the wind changing direction. A long grayish-white funnel was developing below the dark clouds.

Oh my God! It was a tornado!

"Belle! Belle! Run Belle! Run to the barn!" she yelled at the tiny figure now far ahead of her. They wouldn't make it to the house and storm cellar in time. Anna heard the fire station's siren going off as she raced towards Belle and the barn, the wind battering her body. She wasn't sure if Belle had heard her screaming. Oh please, she had to catch her!

She squinted through the rain and wind as Belle ran into the barn. It took all the strength to fight the wind and follow her inside.

"Belle! Come to me and hold on!" she called.

Belle was soaking wet, her red shirt and jeans plastered to her tiny shivering body. She ran to Anna sobbing in fright. Anna grabbed her grandchild and looked around frantically for a place to shelter them. As she raced towards the sturdy pole in the center of the barn, the twister hit the farm.

The sound of the tornado hitting the ground was like several jet planes all taking off at the same time. In a ferocious roar of noise and destruction the old barn came apart, the wood splintering into thousands of big and small weapons as each piece was hurtled into the air as if shot out of a cannon. Anna tried to hold onto Belle as hard as she could, but the powerful winds wrenched her precious bundle from her arms.

"No!" Anna screamed as Belle was lifted like a rag doll into the air. Anna felt herself rising and spinning, being hurled into dark depths of wind and battering rain. She was tossed and turned and slammed into the ground. Then there was nothing but blackness.

Anna dreamed she was back in Jane's car the day of her 50th birthday. She was laughing about something Jane was telling her. All of a sudden another car smashed into them, and she felt her body rising above the car and then shooting through an all encasing blackness. She was hurtled faster and faster through this dark space, images coming at her like a brilliant meteor shower passing by. Images of herself as a little girl, as a teenager and a grown woman, her whole life flying past her in seconds. She squeezed her eyes shut and felt terror and confusion threatening to overwhelm her. Her body came to a swift, jerking stop. Anna opened her eyes and she was again standing on a hill overlooking the strange valley and town. The gray-haired lady was standing beside her, looking at her with a serious expression on her face. "It's time Anna," she told her firmly.

"Anna! Anna!"

She heard Eric calling her name through the swirling black fog in her head, his voice tinged with fear.

"Anna! Save Belle! You have to save her!"

Belle! Anna opened her eyes wide. She lifted her head from the debris all around her and wiped the dirt and rain off her face. There was total destruction as far as she could see. There was nothing left of the house or barn. The tornado had cut a deep track, taking out everything in its path.

"Belle! Belle! Where are you?!" Anna screamed. She tried to get to her feet, but fell to her knees in pain. Her side was burning in agony. She placed her hand over it and saw gushing blood. Anna got to her feet again. She had to find Belle!

"Anna, find Belle! Save Belle!" Eric was still yelling to her but she couldn't see him or tell where he was.

"Belle! Please! Where are you?"

A field of debris lay scattered everywhere. It looked as though a bomb had gone off. She ran as fast as she could, calling her granddaughter. Finally she spotted the red shirt. Anna grabbed her side and sped towards it.

"Belle! I'm here Belle!" Anna screamed as she tossed a huge piece of splintered board off of her granddaughter's prone form. The tiny body looked broken.

No! She would not let this happen! She anxiously bent down and brushed Belle's drenched hair away from her pale face. Her eyes were closed. Her tiny lips tinged blue. Anna searched for a pulse on her wrist, then placed her hand over Belle's small heart. And there it was. She was alive! Anna knew she didn't have much time. She could hear sirens coming closer but she also felt with her whole being that they would not make it in time to save Belle.

Somehow, she found her hands frantically searching for the pendant she wore around her neck. Thank goodness it was still there! She pulled the necklace over her head and grasped the pendant between her fingers. Her hands were wet with the blood from her injured side so it took precious moments to open the clasp that held the capsule. After taking deep breaths to calm herself, she lifted the tiny blue capsule out of its bed and grasped it between her thumb and forefinger. She didn't really know why she was doing this, but as she looked at Belle's tiny body she just knew she had to trust her impulse. Anna opened Belle's mouth and placed the capsule behind her tongue. She closed the small lips and gently caressed her granddaughter's arm. She was such a baby, she thought. Please let it work!

Anna sobbed and prayed, wishing she could take Belle into her arms but not daring to move her. She could still hear the sirens, and people's voices, but she concentrated all her attention on Belle. Everything inside Anna stopped. The sounds disappeared and a feeling of serenity and calmness came over her. She thought about nothing else except the life of this precious child with a face so much like Andy's.

Andy. Suddenly, she remembered the last few days of his life. She had sat at his bedside reading and talking to him. Telling him stories. He had been unconscious for days. She struggled to remember the last thing he had said to her but she couldn't. When he finally died, she'd been holding his right hand and his left had been on his chest.

Anna looked down at the pendant that she'd dropped on Belle's chest. It was lying upside down beside her tiny hand. As she gazed at her granddaughters miniscule fingers she noticed the sign Belle seemed to be making. "I love you". Now, she knew. It was the same shape that Andy's left hand had been making when he took his final breath. Andy *had* been trying to talk to her! He had made the only gesture he was able to.

As Anna reached out and caressed her small hand, Belle's chest began to visibly rise and fall. Her face began to regain color, her tiny body no longer looked broken! Anna could not save her beloved Andy, but somehow, someway, she had saved her grandchild.

Belle opened her blue eyes. "Don't cry Anna-gram." she whispered.

Anna sobbed and reached out and gathered Belle close to her.

"Are you alright, sweetheart?" she asked her anxiously. She patted her body with gently probing hands. There seemed to be no injuries at all!!

But then she remembered. Eric. He'd called to her so urgently. Had he made it through as well?

"Listen to me Belle," she said. "Can you sit here and wait for Uncle Eddie and the firemen? I need to find Eric."

She kissed her granddaughter's damp hair and stood up. Her side hurt badly and the blood was beginning to trickle onto her jeans.

Anna looked around anxiously at the pile of splintered barn rubble. She had concentrated so hard on saving her granddaughter that she had not heard a word from Eric since he had screamed at her to save Belle.

"Eric! Eric! Where are you?" she called.

God, there was such destruction! The farm that had been in her family for over 150 years had been destroyed in an instant, ripped apart by nature's fury. She carefully walked through the debris until she found the heap of wood that looked like it had once been the farm house. She spotted the splintered remnants of its front door, there was an arm sticking out from under it.

Eric!

Anna grabbed the edge of the broken door and tried to push it off him, but there was too much debris piled on top of it. It was so heavy! She bent down and touched Eric's face.

"Can you hear me?" she called to him, wiping off his face with her wet t-shirt.

Eric slowly opened his eyes and looked at Anna as though trying to bring her face into focus. His face was plastered with mud and rain. A small trickle of blood ran from his forehead.

"Did you save Belle?" she heard him whisper.

Anna leaned close to hear him. "Yes, I saved her," she told him.

Eric smiled. "I'm glad Anna. That's what you needed to do."

Anna's hand went to the pendant she she'd jammed in her pocket, and the tears came. She only had that one capsule. She could only save one life.

"Help! Help us!" she yelled out toward the road. She saw a fire truck coming up the long driveway. "They're, coming Eric. They will help you. Just hold on OK?"

"Anna, come here and lie down beside me," he said.

Anna was so tired. She was starting to feel the loss of blood. Her breathing was coming in labored gasps. When she took a deep breath her chest pounded and a vise of pain spread across her sides. She stumbled to sit down and laid as close as she could to him, and put her arm across his chest, her head on his shoulder. She kissed his face. Eric was such a good man. She couldn't endure another loss to her already slowly mended heart! He was so special to her, his unconditional love had taken away so much of the sadness inside her. His smile and laughter lit up her life. This man was such a wonderful gift.

"Will you marry me, Eric?"

"Your timing is terrible," he said with a short laugh and gasp of pain."Yes, I will."

"I love you Eric," she said.

"I love you too, Anna. I'll see you again real soon, OK?"

"Promise?"

"I promise."

Anna kissed him gently, her tears landing on his pale face. She laid her head on his chest and closed her eyes at the pain in her heart and her body and struggled to open them. She watched the firemen coming. Her vision blurred as she saw a man crossing what was left of the yard. He picked up Belle and hugged her to him and then put her down and looked toward Anna.

"Anna! Anna!" It was Eddie, running towards her. His deep voice was unmistakable. Anna hoped somehow in all this debris her family would find her journals and understand what had happened to her during those nine missing days. She hoped that they would finally find answers to all their questions.

She tried to answer him, but she was suddenly so tired. She knew she'd feel better if she could just lie there and rest for awhile. She closed her eyes.

"Anna! Anna!

Then louder. "Anna!"

CHAPTER TWENTY EIGHT

"Anna! Anna!"

"Anna! Wake up, Anna!"

Anna felt herself being shaken. She tried to open her eyes but they felt so heavy. There was a pounding in her head that drummed persistently against her temples. The pain of it made her grimace, but she focused on opening her eyes.

She could see a white wall in front of her. On the wall was a large clock with black numbers. The time it showed was 12:12. She moved her eyes carefully around the room, blinking back the dryness. Her eyes felt like sandpaper. The place she was in looked like a hospital room.

She felt her shoulder being shaken gently and turned to see Eddie standing beside the bed. He was mouthing words instead of speaking them, which she found puzzling. She thought he was soundlessly saying, "You are going to be OK, Anna." She shook her head again, trying to clear it.

Eddie shook her shoulder again and she turned to look back at him. His face was worn and exhausted. He had shadows under his eyes and looked as if he hadn't shaved in days.

"*You are going to be OK,*" he mouthed again and signed.

Signed! Eddie was signing to her! It came to her all at once like she'd run smack into a wall. She couldn't hear! Her breath began coming in heaving gasps. Nothing in the room made noise!

"Eddie?" she said tentatively and there it was again! She couldn't hear herself talking. "Eddie!" Her voice rose in a panicked scream that she didn't hear.

"Anna! Look at me, look at me!" Eddie put his hands on her face and tried to calm her. "You are going to be fine." He was talking in the slow careful way he had used since she was 16 years old.

"I can't hear you, Eddie!" she yelled to him as tears ran down her face. She frantically reached up and touched the area above her left ear. The implant was exactly where it had been since she was 18 years old!

Eddie looked at her in confusion.

"Where is Belle and Eric?" she asked him, grabbing his hand.

"Anna, I don't understand. Who are Belle and Eric?'

Anna felt her chest tighten, as fear shot through her body.

Eddie tried to soothe her, but she was sobbing and shaking so much that he pulled her to him and hugged her tight, trying to calm her. He held her until he felt the tears and shaking subside and he laid her head back on her pillow. Her face was white and terrified.

Eddie talked to her slowly. "Anna, you were in a car accident. You were seriously hurt and in a coma for almost nine days. You are going to be alright now. The worst has passed."

Anna couldn't believe what he was saying. The car accident had happened years ago! She had disappeared!

"What day is it?" she asked him in a dry whisper as he leaned down to hear her. Her throat hurt. It was so difficult to talk.

He frowned again. "It's December 21st, Anna," he told her and watched her shake her head. "December 21st, 2012."

Anna gasped. "No," she whispered.

"Anna, look at me. You were in a car accident on your birthday. You were in the passenger side of Jane's car as she was driving downtown to take you to lunch. Her car was broadsided by another vehicle that ran a red light and hit it head on. You were badly hurt and in a coma for nine days," he told her.

Eddie didn't tell her then that her heart had stopped beating for almost a minute after she was brought to the emergency room. The doctors and nurses had worked frantically to save her life. She'd been put into a drug-induced coma to protect her injured brain from swelling.

Anna turned away from him as the tears continued to fall. It had never happened! Her disappearance and reappearance and her time at this other planet in the future. She never regained her hearing. Oh God, Belle! Belle had never existed. She and Eric had been figments of her injured imagination.

Allyson came into the room carrying two cups of coffee. When she saw her mother, the tiredness in her face changed to pure joy. She put the coffee down and rushed to hug Anna.

"Oh Mom! Thank God!"

Anna watched her beloved daughters face and read her lips. The shock at not being able to hear her voice tore at Anna's heart as she hugged her close. She lay back on the pillow, her head pounding, and clutched Allyson's hand.

"I could hear your wonderful voice, Allyson," she said. "It was just the way I had always imagined it would be!" She smiled shakily at her daughter as Allyson looked back at her in surprise.

"I could hear you again too, Eddie. I could hear Jane as well," she said and turned to look at her brother.

Allyson and Eddie glanced at each other with alarm.

"It was wonderful to hear again. My family, music and birds. The rain and the wind. Certain things that I could never forget," she told them.

"You were married to Mark Browning and had a baby girl named Annabelle," she said to Allyson, who looked back at her in shock.

Allyson and Mark had married in the family church in town. Allyson had been wearing Anna's own wedding dress and her grandmothers veil. Eddie had walked his niece down the aisle. Hadn't all that really happened?

How could Annabelle not be real? Hadn't she been there when she was born and watched her take her first breath? Hadn't she heard her little girl voice and giggles as they talked to each other? And the anxiety and heartbreak, then the incredible joy, when she was saving Belle during that tornado. How could none of that be real? She remembered that day of her 59th birthday and looking around her home at all the framed photographs of her grandchild. Moments in her tiny lifetime. Yet, those moments never took place.

"Belle" Anna whispered.

***

Early the next morning, Anna lay watching her daughter sleeping in the hospital chair beside her bed. It had been several hours now since she had awaken from her coma. The doctors had come in and checked her thoroughly and said she would continue to heal and recover.

Anna encouraged her family to go home but Allyson wouldn't hear of it. Neither would Eddie. Jane had come by last night and run tearfully into the room to hug her sister-in-law as tightly as she could. They had talked for awhile while Eddie had gone to the cafeteria to take a break. Poor Jane's face was severely bruised and her broken nose still bandaged. Both of her eyes were blackened. It was stark evidence that they had indeed been in that car accident just days before.

Now Eddie was sitting on the other side of her bed watching her. Anna knew it was no use telling him to go home and get some sleep. Jane had gone to the cafeteria.

Eddie reached out and touched her arm. *"Do you want to talk about it?"* he signed.

Anna took a deep sigh. "I am not even that upset about the deafness. It hurts but it's been part of my life for 34 years. I guess I'd finally embraced it after all," she said. "I feel disappointment and sadness but I can't help but also feel that it was all a gift. A gift that was given to me somehow for a time. It felt so real." Her eyes settled on the wall clock.

"It's all been going over and over it in my mind. It's still so confusing but I keep thinking back to the things I remembered 'hearing' again," she whispered. "I can see now that these things I heard were things that I used to be able to hear until I was 16. The music I listened to was always something from my past. The music on the piano that I played was music I played as a young girl and some other sounds I heard, like the birds and sounds of rain, were all from memory. I knew your voice of course, and my family's. The other voices I heard were just from my imagination of how I thought they sounded. I remember thinking that there were huge gaps in what happened during those 'nine years' that passed. There were certain things like Allyson's wedding and the birth of her daughter that I could recall but I didn't have other real memories like other birthdays or holidays in between. I guess that's why I thought the years had passed by so quickly." she said sadly.

And how could she also have only imagined that futuristic town in that beautiful valley? As she'd stood on that hill with the gray-haired lady she had felt the sun on her face and the breeze against her hair. She'd held that pendant firmly in her hands and worn it around her neck, yet none of it ever happened.

"Do you want to talk about 'Eric'?" Eddie said.

Anna shook her head. How could she have made this man up? She had kissed him and felt his arms around her. The long conversations they'd had and the friendship that had turned into real love. She had felt the goodness in his heart and his kind, gentle nature. She had looked into his intense eyes and *known* him. It was still difficult to grasp that he was part of her imagination. It would take a long time to heal from not really ever knowing Eric.

CHAPTER TWENTY NINE
ONE YEAR LATER

As Anna waited for her coffee, she looked around at the bookstore and brushed her hair away from her eyes. The store was decorated for Christmas. Lights and tinsel and bows and ribbons were everywhere. Christmas books were displayed on colorful tables and quite a few people browsed the aisles of row after row of bookcases. In addition to the library where she worked, the bookstore was one of Anna's favorite places to be.

She'd spent the past year healing both physically and emotionally. After waking, there had been another two weeks in the hospital followed by months of outpatient therapy. In the beginning her memory of certain things was sketchy but over the next several months she finally had filled in the gaps in her life. She remembered those three years after Andy died. They were difficult memories to process. The sadness and loneliness and anger was so prominent in her life during that time.

Allyson and Anna's relationship had changed, and for the better. They were finally able to let their shared sorrow over Andy's loss bring them together instead of tearing them apart.

When Allyson graduated from college she came home to live with her. She worked at a teaching hospital in nearby Carmel, and everything seemed to get back to "normal," but Anna wasn't the same as she'd been before the accident...she was better. She was finally able to think of Andy and not break down in tears. She would always miss him, but the pain inside herself at his loss had become a dull ache that she could live with.

Anna had surprised her family by telling them she planned to move out to the farmhouse in spring. She was full of plans for the farm and hopes for its future. Inspired by the dreams about solar energy and farming, she had taken it upon herself to learn everything she could about it. She was determined to use this knowledge to carry her family's farming history into the future.

She'd run into Mark Browning during the summer and invited him to dinner with her and Allyson. Anna chuckled as she remembered her daughter's surprise and red face when she'd showed up with Mark. She clearly remembered what Anna had told her in the hospital about the two of them as a couple when she came out of her coma. Allyson had spent much of the dinner glowering at her while Anna looked back at her innocently. But the two had genuinely seemed to like each other and over the last several months had begun to date. Anna didn't know what would become of it, but she had hope for their future.

A cheerful barista wearing an elf hat waved at Anna and put up a finger to show "one moment". Anna nodded at her and looked around at the room to distract herself. It was filled with display cases of movies and her eyes lit on a copy of the classic "The Wizard of Oz", which made her smile sadly. The tornado that had shattered her home had been part of her imagination. How real it had seemed, the incredible noise and roaring that shook the very ground. The hail and wind that had buffered her body and tossed her like a plastic toy. The destruction seen through her eyes after it had hit the farm was like nothing she could possible imagine. Yet she *had* imagined it all. Anna sighed. Just a dream.

The barista held Anna's coffee toward her and wished her a "Merry Christmas". Anna signed 'thank you' to her, and carrying her coffee and the bag of books she had purchased earlier, threaded her way towards the only empty table in the room.

As she moved past an occupied table towards the next available empty one she casually looked at the man sitting at it. The first thing she noticed about him was his blondish gray hair. When she got close enough to see his face, she felt the hairs on her neck stand up.

It was Eric!

Anna stumbled and caught the edge of his table. He looked up at her in surprise.

So swiftly her coffee tumbled towards him, Anna sat down on the other chair at his table. Fortunately, he caught it before it could spill the hot liquid all over himself.

She sat there staring at him wordlessly.

"Are you alright Ma'am?" he asked her, concerned by her strange behavior.

Anna tried to calm her breathing before he thought he'd need to call 911. As she stared at him, she began to notice subtle differences between this man and the Eric she had dreamed of. His eyes were not blue like the man she had imagined, but light brown or hazel. His hair was longer and styled differently. There was a cleft in his chin and he was wearing a black suit and dark gray tie. His overall look was of a man who was very polished and professional, not the farmer Eric she'd dreamed. She remembered during her dreams when she had compared the photographs of Belle and Andy as babies. This was the way she felt now. There were incredible similarities, yet not exactly the same.

But she also saw kindness and warmth on his face even though he was looking at her warily.

"What..what's your name?" Anna asked him, almost stumbling over her words. He frowned slightly. Whether at her question or her speech, she wasn't sure.

"Michael."

He wiped up the small bit of spilled coffee from her cup and finally gave her a tentative smile.

There was something in the way that he looked at her that started to melt the eternal cold she had felt so long around her heart.

"Michael, I'm Anna," she said reached out and offered her hand.

He gave her a much bigger smile, showing perfect white teeth.

"It's nice to meet you, Anna," he said taking her hand in his and shaking it gently.

"So, Michael. Do you have time to hear a story?" she asked him, finally releasing his well manicured hand.

"What's your story about, Anna?" he asked her slowly.

Anna shrugged off her coat and set down her book bag and purse on the table. Again, she felt a tingle of awareness as she looked at his face. Yeah, maybe he'd think she was crazy. But, maybe not. How many chances did one get in life? She knew she had to take this one.

She started out her story slowly, but gained more confidence as she continued. "It was my 50th birthday. My sister-in-law Jane and I were riding in her car as she drove me to lunch. There was a terrible accident and somehow, some way, I disappeared right from the car and no one could find me."

As she spoke, everyone else in the bookstore seemed to fade into the background. It was just the two of them.

"You don't look anywhere near 50," Michael told her with a devilish grin.

Anna felt herself blushing.

"That's a pretty good story so far," he said. "What happened next?"

Anna took a sip of her coffee. "The weather was overcast and cold that day. It was raining just like today..."

***

Outside the bookstore window a lovely gray-haired lady stood watching the couple at the table. She was wearing a very modern gray suit and dark overcoat. She smiled as the two of them laughed together, her blue eyes crinkling at the corners. She put down the umbrella she was holding and slowly reached up and touched the intricately designed pendant she wore around her neck. She ran her forefinger over the light blue stone at its center and for just a moment, the stone glowed and seemed to come to life.

Suddenly the rain came to a stop and the clouds parted to reveal a perfect rainbow. The lady took one last glance at the couple, smiled with satisfaction, closed her umbrella, and walked away.

EPILOGUE

There have been two times in my mother's life that she has died. The first time, she was just sixteen years old. Her heart had actually stopped beating for thirty nine seconds. Of course she did recover from that first time or I wouldn't be here to tell you this story. The story of how my mother died on her 50th birthday.

This book has taken me three years to write. I set out to change the end to my mother's life. So much of this story really happened. My mother and Uncle Eddie growing up and my grandparents background is real history. My mother's loss of her hearing when she was sixteen years old and how she coped with being deaf did happen. How my parents met in college and later married and had me, all of that was real. My dad, Andy, and how he died and the grief that my mother and I went through was real.

It was also true that my mother and I grew distant after his death and saw each other less and less. The guilt I felt, and still feel, stays with me to this day that we let the loss become a wedge between us. It wasn't a wedge born of anger or dislike or anything bad. It was a wedge born from grief and constantly being reminded of that loss every time we saw each other. There is no time limit on grief over losing someone you love. It is something that stays with you forever. You learn to get up each day and do what you need to do. You can find a type of peace in remembering their life and that's what I tried to do here. Find peace.

Most of all, the stories my mother told me as a little girl growing up were all true. The stories she shared with my dad throughout their marriage and his illness were stories from her heart and imagination. She told them to us to cheer us up or make us feel better in difficult times or when we just needed a laugh or to smile. It will forever stay with me the pleasure it gave her to share her stories with us and the happiness that shown in her beautiful face at our reactions. My little girl giggles and small hands clapping over favorite stories or my dad Andy's laughing out loud in amusement to her tall tales. It never mattered that she couldn't hear the sound, our expressions shown our joy and delight in each story.

Sometimes the simplest explanation is the right one. My mother Anna Anderson died on December 12th, 2012 at 12:12 pm in an accident in the town she grew up in as my Aunt Jane drove her car through the intersection on Main Street. She was killed instantly. She'd simply been at the wrong place at the wrong time. There was no disappearance and there was no coma. The future tornado in my hometown of Greenway, Indiana in 2021 is just a story.

The day that my Uncle Eddie stood on the porch of my boarding house at college on December 12th, was a real moment. However, he was not there to tell me that my mother had disappeared. He didn't even have to say a thing. I knew from the look on his face as I walked towards him that my mother had died. It is a moment that haunts my dreams, even now.

The time and date of the accident never left my thoughts. I would see this date over and over in my mind as if it had become tattooed on my soul. I would constantly look at clocks and no matter what the time actually was, all I could see was 12:12. At times the date stayed with me like a loud drum banging in the same room. I couldn't escape the noise. As I started to write this story the sound lessened more and more and instead of the incessant drum beats, I would began to hear the soothing musical tones of my mom Anna, playing her beloved piano. Just like she did as a teenager, like I imagined she still did. Her music telling its own story with each lyrical melody. As I closed my eyes and listened, I felt the ache in my heart lessen. The date and time would become the center of this book. It became, in a sense, not just my mother's story but a book about timing in life and second chances.

One of the most challenging parts of writing this story was writing it from the perspective of a deaf person. Not only that, but from the point of view of a deaf person who regains the gift of sound. I had been around deafness my whole life but I didn't really know what it was like to cope with it constantly, to not be able to hear at all. It was here when I felt myself struggling to explain these feelings and emotions, that I felt my mom's presence the most. I believe that these words are hers and that I was only the instrument to put them to paper.

I wrote so many things that I wish I had told my mom, the conversations we never got to have. In my story we talked of our pain and grief over my dad's passing. We shared more laughter and tears, jokes and stories and hugs. I shared with her my feelings of falling in love and the wedding she never got to attend. My "if only" became a perception of reality as I wrote each chapter. I found my own way to share these with her, the way she truly could understand, through the written word.

I could have ended this story in so many different ways. I could have ended it in the year 2021 after my mom "saved" Annabelle during the tornado. I could have ended it when she woke up from a coma nine days after the accident. Each time a chapter ended, I felt like I needed to go on, that her story had more chapters and more beginnings. My last chapter of her in the bookstore gave promise to a whole new life for her.

I always thought that if my mother had lived, that she would fall in love again because that would be what my dad, Andy, would have wanted for her. He was the most selfless person I have ever known and he'd have wanted her to be happy, to smile and laugh again and to find love. Eric/Michael became the man I wished she'd have found. The kind of man that she'd have been happy with and I could sense my dad approving of. I chose to have him live on as well in the last chapter. He is the part of my mom's adventure that goes on.

Another part of my story is true. I did marry Mark Browning. He became my strength and anchor when my whole world crumbled around me. When I felt like I had lost everything that mattered to me, he became a new beginning for me as well. Uncle Eddie and Aunt Jane also became a lifeline for me to hang onto. They wouldn't let me stay in the depths of despair and overwhelming sadness that losing both my parents left inside me. I know that neither of them has given into their own grief that they have felt over my mom's accident. I can see the toll that has taken on both of them and the heartbreaking sorrow I see etched in their faces. I know they try to be strong for me, so in my own way, I wrote this story for them too. I gave each of them more time with my mom, to say and do so many things they'd never gotten the chance to. I hope it can comfort them and even bring a smile or a laugh or two and lessen that sadness for awhile.

There is a saying that "everyone dies but not everyone really lives." I have learned in the last six years with the loss of both my parents that no one truly dies if you keep them in your heart and memories forever. Let those memories of moments of love, laughter, tears and joy live on in the thoughts and actions of your everyday lives. Let their stories continue on in your children and grandchildren and all that come after.

Mark and I have a baby girl now that's just six months old. Her name is Annabelle. I will share my mom Anna's stories with her and even make up some of my own. Stories that I did not know I had in me until I began writing this book and felt my mother's soothing presence. In that way, she will never leave me and she will live on in the grandchild she has never met, except only in my imagination.

Allyson Anderson Browning

About the book & the Author

This is my first novel. In order to write this, I needed to have traveled down that road of personal growth to gain both physical and intellectual life experiences. I needed to have moments of great happiness and inconsolable grief to shape the person that I have become. It was my time.

Almost every writer, editor or professional that gives you advice about writing fiction will tell you one of the first rules is "don't make it personal". I not only made my main character Anna Anderson personal by having her not only be deaf, but lose her hearing from meningitis...just as I did at age twelve.

When I first wrote the outline for this story, there was no "Epilogue". As I wrote and got to truly know and understand each of my characters, my story took a different direction. I asked myself constantly "How can I end this story in a way that's logical?" Even though it's fiction, it still needs to be plausible and believable. The answer was to have it not be Anna Anderson's second chance, but her daughter Allyson's. Allyson wrote this book in her mother's memory and as a way to cope with her grief. There are numerous clues throughout this book that it would end the way that it did. I encourage you to go back and find them.

Even more personal is that I wrote this book for my children who lost their father in a tragic accident. I've tried to give comfort to my family who have been through so much heartache, especially to my parents who've lost two sons and two grandsons. For those of you who have ever lost a loved one through sickness or terrible circumstances, and for those of you who still grieve over the passing of someone you loved, this book is for you as well.

As I wrote this book, I felt memories of lost loved ones overwhelm me. Each one of us have asked ourselves at least once "what if I had a second chance?". Writing this novel helped me to focus on the wonderful moments that each loved one brought into my life. Each of them was a gift that I was given for a time and timing was indeed everything. I truly began to feel my own heart healing by the end of this story.

If I can touch just one of you with my written words, then I will have accomplished what I set out to do.

***

Constance Flamion is a native of Elkhart, Indiana. She currently lives in the mountains of north Georgia. You can contact her at: synchronicityanna@gmail.com.

Made in the USA
Charleston, SC
16 October 2015